D1083276

Quadriphobia

Quadriphobia

ALAN RYAN

DOUBLEDAY & COMPANY, INC.

GARDEN CITY, NEW YORK

1986

"Kiss the Vampire Goodbye" copyright © 1985, 1986 by Alan Ryan (First published in *Alfred Hitchcock's Mystery Magazine,* June 1985).

"The Man Who Killed Forever" copyright © 1986 by Alan Ryan.

"Candlewyck" copyright © 1986 by Alan Ryan.

"The Queen of Kilimanjaro" copyright © 1986 by Alan Ryan.

Library of Congress Cataloging-in-Publication Data

Ryan, Alan, 1943–
    Quadriphobia.

    Contents: Kiss the vampire goodbye—The man who
killed forever—Candlewyck—[etc.]
    1. Horror tales, American. I. Title.
PS3568.Y26Q3   1986   813'.54   85-20451
ISBN 0-385-19839-6

To John Barleycorn

and to Pat,
who never slanches

Cheers!

Contents

Kiss the Vampire Goodbye

I never believed in ghosts or vampires or zombies or anything like that. I always thought that stuff was silly, maybe good enough to entertain women and children with a harmless little scare, but there was nothing in it for a private investigator trying to make an honest living. That's what I try to do. I try to make an honest living—honest enough to let me sleep soundly at night and enough of a living to keep the rent paid on a cheap apartment in West L.A. and a two-room office downtown, with maybe a little left over for a drink at night to help me forget the kind of people I have to deal with during the day. So when Mary Cantrell showed up in my office one afternoon and told me her father had been killed by a vampire, I nearly told her to take a walk.

She looked like what used to be called "a pretty little thing," back in the days when you could describe a woman that way and not get your block knocked off. What I mean is, she wasn't one of your modern, super-liberated women, all hard bony edges and a chip on her shoulder—not Mary Cantrell. She was little enough, maybe five two, and she was pretty, nobody could argue with that. I pegged her at twenty-three. Black hair tied up on her head in some way that's a mystery to men, except you know that if she ever lets it down around her shoulders, you better hold onto your heart and start taking some very deep breaths. Skin like milk. And those eyes. Those eyes were so dark and deep that you wanted to crawl inside right through them and be safe and secure for the rest of your life. I thought I could see in those eyes and in the way she held her head a kind of diamond-like quality, a nerve, a kind of spunkiness, a hardness in the center. She was wearing a dark blue skirt and a plain white blouse, no jewelry. She didn't need jewelry. She had those eyes. I liked her.

"I need your help, Mr. Kendall," she said.

"Where did you hear about me?"

Her eyes didn't waver at the question. That's something I watch for.

"The phone book," she said. "The yellow pages."

People say that to me more often than you'd think. So I looked her over, nodded, and I let her talk.

While she told me her story, I sat at my desk moving papers around as if I had an overwhelming load of urgent cases. And the more I listened, the more I realized that Mary Cantrell's spunkiness was definitely riding in the back seat today. She was scared, badly scared. And when a spunky girl gets scared, I get interested.

When she was done, I didn't let any expression show in my face. I said, "Tell me again. Go more slowly this time. Tell it in order and tell me everything."

"Aren't you going to write anything down?" she asked. She was looking at the expanse of bare, scarred wood I had cleared on the desk in front of me. Despite her grief at her father's death, and despite the scare that had sent her looking for me in the first place, she was thinking clearly.

"Don't worry about it," I told her. "I have a memory like a banker." That wasn't a good thing to say because her father, recently deceased, had been a banker. I didn't know that until she started the story again.

She looked at me closely for a few seconds, studying my face, and then obviously reached a decision.

"All right," she said, in a very businesslike sort of way. Not only did I like this girl, I was already beginning to admire her. And even if her story sounded crazy, she might just be able to make me believe it.

"My name is Mary Cantrell," she began. "My father is . . . my father *was* Jonathan David Cantrell, the founder of California Trade Enterprises, with headquarters in Santa Barbara. Are you familiar with it?"

"They own the California Trade Bank?"

"Yes."

"Even as we speak, I owe CTB fourteen hundred ninety-two dollars, give or take some change. We share ownership of a car."

She didn't blink.

"My father was a multimillionaire."

She said it the way you might mention that your dad had always been pretty good at tying bows on Christmas packages.

"My mother died giving birth to me. I was always the light of my father's life, the living image of my mother, my father always said, and he raised me himself. With the help of our servants, of course."

"Of course," I said.

She heard the tone in my voice because I'd intended her to hear it. She hesitated for a fraction of a second, her eyes meeting mine, then decided to ignore it. That was good because, in the instant our eyes met, we both realized we'd been testing each other. We both passed the test.

"Despite the fact that my father never remarried, and I know he was very often lonely, ours was always a happy home. He and I were devoted to each other, and the servants have been with us for so many years that they're all like my own family."

"Any other family?"

"None," she answered at once. "Both my parents were only children. I'm the last in the line," she said, her voice wavering for the first time, "so the Cantrell name dies with me."

She suddenly looked as if she thought that might happen sometime soon.

"Go on," I told her. I sat back in my chair, trying not to make it squeak the way it usually does. I wanted to signal to her that I was satisfied she could tell the story straight, with all the good bits included, and I wouldn't interrupt again.

She got the message. She didn't fidget while she talked. She concentrated. Her eyes stayed fixed on that bare patch on my desk, as if the drama of her life was being reenacted there in front of her and all she had to do was watch it and describe what happened.

"My father was always a very successful man, but he never sought any of the notoriety that often goes with success. He had no desire whatsoever to be in the public eye, no desire to show off his wealth, no political ambitions. I know that in his earlier years he turned down many opportunities, and people, business acquaintances, still sometimes came to him with offers while I was growing up, but he always refused. He was good at what he did. He was a genius at it, building companies and trading, and knowing that, seeing his enterprises grow and prosper, was satisfaction enough for him.

"He built Kirkdale for my mother forty years ago, up in the hills, and he kept it absolutely private. It was always our home and nothing else. I grew up there and I love it as much as I loved my father. No one was ever permitted to intrude at Kirkdale. The house itself is a work of art, the view of the hills and the ocean is magnificent, the sunsets take your breath away, and the gardens could win prizes anywhere in the world.

"But Kirkdale was ours and ours alone. He never brought work home with him. He never held meetings there, and no one from the office was even permitted to call him there. He always handled his business so carefully that no crisis could ever intrude on his private life. He even entertained elsewhere, so that strangers never even saw the estate. Only once, about seven years ago, he permitted a photographer from *Paris Match* to take pictures of the garden. It was a favor, really, to some French businessman, but my father always regretted it. We were besieged with requests after that. They were all refused.

"I'm telling you this as background, so you'll understand the context of what happened last night and this morning. Shall I go on?"

I slid a little lower in the chair. It squeaked but we both ignored it.

"There are nine servants at Kirkdale. Most of them have been with my father all of my life. The others were all screened more thoroughly than you'd think possible before they were hired. I'd trust any of them with my life. So did my father."

"Your father's dead," I said. When you have a suspicious mind, there are times when you can't keep your big mouth shut.

She pressed her lips together for a second. Ordinarily they were very pink. Now they turned white.

"Let me tell you the rest," she said. "This morning, my father didn't appear for breakfast. That happened rarely, but it did happen sometimes, so I didn't think much of it. He was getting on in years, and he was beginning to slow down a little. But when he hadn't come down by nine o'clock, I went up to his room. It was empty. The bed hadn't been slept in. I immediately had the servants search the house, and when he wasn't there, we searched all the grounds. The estate is very large and it took a while, about an hour, in fact, but we found him. He was in the rose garden. He . . . was dead, lying on the ground. At first I thought he'd had a stroke or a heart attack. I thought he must have gone out for some air and fallen right where he was, into a tangled plot of rosebushes. He was caught in the branches and tangled up in the thorns very badly."

She stopped for a moment and dropped her gaze onto the hands knotted in her lap. I waited. Then she sighed and raised her head again.

"What else was there to think? He must have just fallen there and gotten tangled. We were all very shaken, but we got him free and carried him inside to the house. I knew he had to die sooner or later, of course, but it was still terrible for me. All the worse, in fact, because his face and hands were badly scratched from the thorns. They're very long, nearly an inch and a half, and I was always warned, by my father and by the servants, to stay away from them when I was little. The bushes require a great deal of attention, too, but the flowers are particularly beautiful. They were my father's favorites in the whole garden, and of course I was struck at once by the irony that it should be in that very place that he died.

"We laid my father's body on the sofa in the library. I sent the servants outside, so that I could be alone with him for a few minutes for the very last time. There was no rush, after all, no family to notify, and the business would go on comfortably without him. He had always planned long ahead and seen to that. I just needed a moment to be alone with him.

"I used my handkerchief to clean a little of the mud from his face and hands. That's when I saw the marks on his throat."

I didn't move. You don't hear a story like this every day, not even in my business.

"There were two deep punctures. At first I thought they were from the thorns, but then I saw they looked different. They were deeper, bigger. The skin was slightly torn, and puffy all around, and a little discolored. I was terrified but I wiped the blood away. I didn't want to believe it, but I was looking right at the marks. There was no other possible explanation."

She was watching me for a reaction. She didn't get one.

"Do you believe me, Mr. Kendall?"

"Finish the story."

"There's not much more to tell. I tried to put that part of it out of my mind for a minute, as best I could. I said goodbye to my father, and then I left the room to give instructions to the staff."

End of story. I looked at her and waited, but that was it.

A vampire. Her father had been bitten and killed by a vampire. The most beautiful girl I have ever been privileged to gaze upon was sitting in front of me, telling me that, and she had come to my office to hire me to track down the vampire and bring him to justice. I have chosen, I told myself for the ten-thousandth time, a very difficult line of work.

I sat up and folded my hands in front of me so they'd cover the worst scars on the desk. My hands have a few scars themselves, but the desk is a lot worse off.

"Who found your father in the rosebushes?" I asked her.

She looked startled, as if a glimmer of something had just appeared to her for the first time. "I did," she said.

"These roses were your father's favorites?"

"Yes."

"And none of the servants thought of looking there?"

"We looked everywhere."

"But the servants didn't look there. How many gardeners are on the staff?"

"Four, and the two outside men help them when necessary."

"That's six."

I thought things over for a while. I wasn't surprised to learn that I hated every bit of it.

"Who inherits?"

"I do."

"What about the servants?"

"They stay on with me, of course."

"Forever?"

"Yes, if they want to. Naturally, my father saw to it they'd be taken care of."

"Maybe *they* took care of *him.*"

She shook her head. I liked the soft way her hair moved. "I couldn't believe a thing like that. You don't know them."

I tried a little smile. It didn't come out very well. "I don't know anything," I told her. "I'm just a blank page, soaking up information, impressions, ideas, waiting to see if any of them make sense. If you're lost in the Sahara and you come to what looks like a road, you figure it's got to go somewhere, right?"

I waited and made her say it. If we pursued this, we might have to go down some dark roads together. I wanted her eyes to be wide open.

"Right," she said, but she made me wait for it. I didn't mind a bit.

"Was your father dressed or wearing a bathrobe?"

"Just a bathrobe. Later, in his bedroom, I saw that the light was on and there was a book beside his chair. He must have gone out for some air after staying up reading."

"Did he do that often?"

"Not often, no, but sometimes."

"His hands and face were covered by scratches from the thorns?"

"Yes."

"And you wiped the blood from them with your handkerchief?"

"The only blood was on the puncture marks." Her eyes didn't waver, not even a little bit.

I was feeling very tired. There wouldn't be blood on the scratches from thorns if he got the scratches after he was dead.

"He was wearing only a bathrobe," I said. "No pajamas?"

"No."

"When he was carried inside, or when he was in the library, did you happen to notice the rest of his body? Maybe you looked for other scratches or marks, something like that."

"I did. There were a few scratches, but I didn't notice anything else."

"How was he lying when you found him?"

"He was face down."

"When you found him, or when you brought him inside, did you see any discoloration, maybe in his face or his chest?"

"No. He was very white. Why? Would that mean something?"

"You don't want to know."

"I do."

She meant it. I kept my voice very even. "If he'd been dead for any length of time, which apparently he was, judging from the bathrobe, the bed, the book, and the light, the blood in his body would have settled to whatever part was lowest. It gets to look sort of purple."

"There was nothing like that," she said. "Nothing like that at all. He was very white. I never thought of anything like that. I didn't know that happened."

She didn't, either. I could see it in her face. And she could see what was in my face. If there had been blood in her father's body after he died, she would have seen the discoloration. No discoloration, therefore no blood. I didn't want to think about the next therefore.

"What about the police?"

She shook her head. "In the first place, they wouldn't believe me. In the second place, I feel obliged to preserve my father's privacy. It's the last thing I can do for him, Mr. Kendall."

"Call me Mike."

When I heard myself say that, I knew I was a goner. She nodded. She knew it too.

"I'll have to see the body."

That was what did it. She stared at me, those eyes almost making my head reel, and then I saw shiny tears welling up in them, threatening to spill out and drown both our hearts.

"You can't," she managed to say.

"Why not?"

"I told you I left him in the library to give instructions to the staff. When I went out, I saw Hawkins, my father's personal servant for more than forty years. I broke down then. I couldn't help it. Hawkins held me for a few minutes—he was always like an uncle to me—until I calmed down. We spoke briefly; then I asked him to call the other servants together and I went back into the library alone. My father's body was gone."

"And the library has at least three doors."

"Four," she said. She sounded about the same way I felt.

"A vampire," I said. I said it very quietly, very flat.

"Yes," she told me.

We looked at each other.

"Will you help me?"

We looked at each other some more.

Finally, she managed a pale and sad little smile, as if she regretted putting this burden on me, but there was strength and growing confidence in it, too. And there were those eyes.

I hadn't seen a pretty girl smile in six weeks, and that was in the movies. It made me want to fix things, shift the world around to where it belonged, so Mary Cantrell could smile like that all the time.

I told her: "I'm your man."

2

It's not every day you meet an albino Eskimo, and very few of the ones you do meet are named Danny Lavender. Nobody smiles when Danny tells them his name.

I met him a few years ago in a pedestrian underpass. He'd just been mugged and he needed a few bucks to get home. All I had was a ten, so I gave it to him. The next afternoon, around the time I usually start contemplating the big dramatic question of the day— beef pot pie or the Hungry Man turkey?—he walked into my office and put a nicely engraved picture of Alexander Hamilton on the desk in front of me.

I stared at the ten for a while, then I stared at him for a while.

"It's a big city," I said when the shock had worn off a little. "How'd you find me?"

He kept his hands folded neatly in his lap.

"I'm here," he said. He didn't say anything else.

"How'd you find me?" I said again. Dogged persistence is one of my long suits.

"I'm good at that sort of thing."

"What do you do for a living?"

"What do you need done?"

I looked him over. I'm no dwarf myself—six feet tall plus a couple more inches I carry with me for emergencies—but it took a while to see all of this guy. If you had to get to the other side of a river, you could walk across on his shoulders. I know a lot of people who don't have a head as big as one of his hands. He was wearing a suit that had forgotten it was ever new around the same time my own suit had lost its memory. He had a scarf around his neck, and he was holding gloves in one hand, a hat, maybe a fedora, in the other. A pair of sunglasses was sticking up from his breast pocket. No sunbathing for this beauty. His skin was as pink as a skinned rabbit's and his hair might have been previously owned by Caspar the Friendly Ghost.

"What's your name?" I said.

He told me. I didn't smile.

"How many guys did it take to mug you?"

"Five," he said. "Plus a couple of blunt instruments."

I made some eye contact with Alexander Hamilton, then I pocketed the ten and stood up.

"Let's go have dinner," I said. "I know a place where the burgers actually had a former association with beef."

We went to Joe's Place. I conduct a lot of my business there, mainly in the line of thinking things over by myself. It's bright, it's clean, the Formica is hardly chipped at all, and you can taste the syrup in the Cokes and the coffee in the coffee.

It's been known to get busy sometimes at lunch, but this was dinnertime. I led the way to my usual table near the wall. I've seen spies do that in the movies, and I figure I'm part of a great tradition. Joe came over himself.

"Hello, Mr. Kendall," he said.

He always calls me Mr. Kendall when I have somebody with me. He knows what I do for a living, and he figures it's a client and the formality makes dining in his establishment a little more elegant. I like Joe.

I ordered for both of us.

While we waited for the burgers, I asked Danny Lavender some questions. He used words as if you had to borrow them from the bank, but he got high marks for his answers.

He told me he was an Eskimo and that he was from the Klondike, which is so far up in Alaska that you don't need to know where it is. He told me he still had family there but he finally had to leave. Too much bright light for an albino.

"So you came to dark and storm-tossed California," I said.

"More buildings," he said. "More night work. I only work at night."

He was right enough about the night work. In a city like Los Angeles, everything, good or bad, top to bottom, depends on night work. Sometimes I think my whole life depends on night work.

I listened to him and I watched him. I liked the sound of his voice and the fact that he only used it as necessary. I liked the way he looked me right in the eye when he talked. I also liked the size of him and the easy way he moved it around. I liked the ten in my pocket and the way he'd found me to return it. I even had a feeling Alex Hamilton would have liked him, too.

I told him: "I might have night work sometimes for an associate."

He looked at me across the table. He wasn't going to ask. I admired that.

"Besides," I said, "I read in a book someplace that all private investigators have to wear hats. I hate wearing a hat."

"I've got a hat."

"You've got a job, too."

Just then, Joe brought the burgers to the table and set them down.

"Joe," I said, "I want you to meet my new associate, Danny Lavender."

Danny stuck out one of his hams and Joe took hold of as much of it as he could grasp.

Within the next year, Danny Lavender saved my neck three times. I buy him a lot of burgers at Joe's Place.

My luck was running high and the car started on the first attempt. I followed Mary Cantrell out of the city and up to Kirkdale. The two cars going up the road like that must have looked like before and after.

I like driving. You can feel the ground beneath you, feel the wind in your face, feel yourself moving forward. It's easy to kid yourself that you're accomplishing something useful, when all you're really doing is driving a car. I didn't know what I was doing that day.

I thought about it and decided that I only believed two things just then. I believed there were no such things as vampires. And I believed Mary Cantrell when she said her father had been killed by one. So I thought about it some more, and decided that I really only believed one thing. I believed those eyes.

We left the coast highway and headed up into the hills. In a few minutes, we were on roads that don't deserve the name.

Then we got to Kirkdale.

It was surrounded by a fence, but the fence was discreetly hidden by trees and bushes. So was the gate. Mary Cantrell must have worked some widget in the car because when we got there a clump of trees very considerately and just as silently slid out of the way for us. When we'd passed through, they glided back into place and pretended they hadn't moved.

There are countries in the UN with less acreage than we passed on the driveway. I should have expected the house, but you never expect a house like that one.

Mary Cantrell had told me it was on top of a hill, but if this hill had come to visit Mohammed, he wouldn't have felt slighted. It was a respectable size, not quite as big as Windsor Castle and with fewer chimneys than Pittsburgh. Gardens and greenhouses stretched away down the hill. From the side of the house where we parked the cars, you could see half the Pacific Ocean. On a clear day, you might even spot hula girls in the distance.

My car was wheezing from the altitude. While it coughed itself into silence, I put my hands on my hips and tried to take in the scene. When I turned back toward the house, a first cousin of Bela Lugosi was standing in the doorway.

Mary Cantrell whispered to me that the Dracula look-alike was Hawkins, her father's personal valet. I decided that if I had to wake up every morning to see him laying out my suit, the only thing I'd have to be grateful for was that I wasn't in it.

It was a nice house. The front entry sent back echoes of our footsteps. If you were a bat, you'd always know where you were.

I'd instructed Mary to tell the staff that I was an insurance investigator. I figured I'd hint to them myself that I had undefined links to the lawyer's office that would be handling the will. That way they should be willing to cooperate and also be on their best behavior. Lawyers and insurance companies are notoriously reluctant to hand out money to the grieving relatives when they can't clap eyes on the corpse.

In a few minutes, Hawkins had assembled the whole staff in the drawing room. They weren't a pretty picture.

I went for the three women first. If that sounds mean, I'll have to live with it. Murder is pretty mean, too.

The cook was Dracula's missus. She looked like she might have an attack of severe *angst* any minute, so I started on her with a sharp jab. "Where's Cantrell's body?"

I said it out of the side of my mouth, the way you see it done in the movies. It's a good technique. People automatically know how they're supposed to react. Mrs. Dracula jumped like she'd just found a spider spinning a web in her mouth. Everybody else froze and looked extremely unhappy. I gave up any hopes of being voted Houseguest of the Year.

"I . . . I don't know."

It was a good answer and the others began to thaw out a little. I came back with more questions, to keep the temperature low, but I didn't expect to learn anything from this session unless one of them tipped something by accident. After about five minutes, I knew they were too good for that, or else they were all innocent. I went on with the questions, seeing to it everybody got a turn to be nervous, but I couldn't hope for anything more than to learn their personalities.

I learned a lot, all of it bad. These people had no loyalty to anyone but themselves. Cantrell had never been anything but a meal ticket to them, and now they were assured of eating regular for the rest of their lives, and doing it in style at Kirkdale. Maybe they weren't vampires, but you don't have to be a vampire to be a bloodsucking freak. I didn't trust them and I didn't like them.

In between questions and answers, I stole a few looks at Mary Cantrell. What I saw made my insides turn into a prizewinning macramé exhibit. She thought they all loved her.

It was a nice afternoon, so I spent a couple of hours by myself, taking the sun and snooping around the gardens and the grounds. All the place needed to qualify as a national park was a souvenir stand and a couple of bears.

Cantrell's favorite roses held my attention for a long time. They were the color of blood an hour after it runs out of a wound. If you were building a house, you could use the thorns and save yourself the price of nails. I looked at those bushes and thought about them for a while, then I decided there was nothing in it for me. Instead, I covered the ground all around them. That's when I found it.

There are clues and there are clues. Some of them only require one look for your day to turn into Christmas. Some of them never say a word to you. This one was the silent type.

It was a piece of dental floss about four inches long.

I kneeled over it as if I were thinking about starting a religion. I didn't touch it for a while, just studied it in its natural state. It was twisted a little, and muddy, but its waxy surface shone in a couple of spots, so there was no mistaking what it was.

After a while, I picked it up and took inventory. I'd been right the first time. It was about four inches long. Johnson & Johnson. Flavored with cinnamon. And maybe with something else. I hoped the brown stains were only mud.

I needed two things very badly, a Baggie and a drink. I only had one of them on me at the moment, so I carefully put the dental floss in my wallet, where there was nothing to contaminate it, and pulled the bottle from its holster under my jacket.

"Are you going to keep that all to yourself?" a voice said softly behind me. It was the kind of voice that makes a man turn around with his eyes wide open.

It was Dracula's daughter, Elvira Hawkins, Mary Cantrell's personal maid and companion. She was wearing a black uniform that didn't insult her figure. It didn't insult my imagination, either. I'd had other things on my mind back in the drawing room, but I'd noticed her. You couldn't miss a profile like that, even in black, maybe especially in black, but I can concentrate on my job when I have to. Now I'd put in a few hours, interviewed possible suspects, inspected the scene of the murder, and filed what could be a clue. I was on my break anyway. I handed over the bottle.

She took it and drank without wiping off the top. That did something to me. I didn't want to admit, even to myself, what it was.

"What did you want to see me about?" I said.

"I'm curious about who you are."

"I'm an insurance investigator. Sometimes I work with lawyers, too. It depends."

"No, you're not. You're not with any insurance company. Insurance investigators have better suits," she said. "So do guys who work with lawyers."

I didn't even blink. "You can't tell by the cut of the cloth," I told her.

"I can," she said. "Only one thing had me puzzled."

"What was that?"

"You don't wear a hat," she said. "Private investigators always wear hats."

I gave her my most winning smile.

"I have a hat. I hate it. I hire a guy to wear it for me."

We grinned at each other for a while.

Then I figured my break was over and I went back to work.

I put my hand out and she put the bottle in it.

"Okay," I said, "I'm an investigator, private or otherwise. Do you have something I might want to investigate, or were you just thirsty?"

At some point in your relationship, a woman who wears black is sure to turn nasty. I've learned that over the years.

"Listen, you shamus or shaman or shogun or whatever you guys are called, you've only horned in here where you're not needed or wanted. Kirkdale has always been safe from people like you. Isn't it bad enough that Mr. Cantrell was bitten by a vampire and murdered right here where he should be safe, in the comfort of his own home? Poor Mary is in her room, crying her eyes out. I've spent my life trying to protect her from the harsh realities of life, just the way her father wanted me to. Now all this has happened. Please, leave her alone! Your help can only make life worse for her, even worse than her father's death has already made it. Leave her alone! Leave us all alone!"

She didn't even say goodbye, but she was nice to look at in that black uniform running up the hill to the house. The only thing that kept me from enjoying the view completely was the fact that neither Mary Cantrell nor I had said word one to the staff about vampires.

I took Mary Cantrell with me when I left that place. She protested a little because she didn't understand why I was so worried about her. I reminded her that she was paying me to tell her things like this, even if she didn't like them. Especially if she didn't like them. She said she'd come with me.

Hawkins saw us to the door, but I could tell from his face that he wasn't hoping we had a nice day.

We left in separate cars. It was a while before we reached civilization. When I saw a diner that looked as if it might have evolved enough to have a telephone, I signaled to Mary and pulled into the parking lot.

"Sit tight," I called across to her. She nodded, looking very unhappy but very brave.

I went in and found the phone and called Danny Lavender.

"I have some night work," I told him. "Meet me at the office at seven. Bring your fists."

When I went back to the parking lot, Mary Cantrell was gone. They'd left her car there, with the driver's door open, as a souvenir.

3

I called Danny Lavender again, then sat by the window in the diner drinking coffee. When I saw Danny's car roll into the parking lot, I signaled to the waitress and ordered two burgers.

He took the hat off but kept the glasses on when he sat down across from me. He didn't say a word, but the angle of his head told me he was eager to hear about the case.

"This one could ruin your appetite," I told him. "Wait till we eat."

The burgers were exactly what I expected. I added another star to the rating of Joe's Place.

We even risked the coffee. It was going to be a long night.

When I told Danny everything that had happened, he still didn't say a word but he nodded three times during the story. When Danny Lavender nods once, that means he thinks the case is really bad. I'd never seen him nod three times. I waved for more coffee and this time I added reinforcements from my holster.

"We have to get her out of there," I said.

Danny Lavender nodded again.

It's like when you see a guy ahead of you on the highway pass an exit, then stop and back up. You don't do anything at first. You just stare at him, trying to comprehend the fact that he's really doing this thing.

That's how it is when you suddenly get a break in a case. It's like the sun deciding to shine in your window at midnight. I stood there on the steps of the diner, staring at Mary Cantrell's car. The same car she'd driven when she led the way up to Kirkdale. The car that had the widget for the gate.

An owl could have found the gate again in about two minutes. To me, every tree looks like every other tree. I like them all right, but they have a tendency to stand between me and where I'm going. When we got to where I thought we were close, we had to kill the headlights and cruise in the dark. It took over an hour to locate that gate in the pitch blackness, with Danny leaning on the widget all the way.

Once we were inside, Danny rigged the widget to keep the gate open while I turned the car around so it faced out toward the road. I like to leave a place quiet and quick.

The moon was high above us by the time we hiked up to the house. When we reached the edge of the woods on one side, Danny pointed up. The whole house was in darkness, just a black shape against the black sky, except for a light in one window on the second floor. While I stood there, trying to convince my lungs to go back to work, I saw a shadow pass the window, then pass it again. I knew that shadow. It was Mary Cantrell.

Then I saw another shadow in the same window. I knew that shadow, too. I would have known it anywhere.

It was Elvira Hawkins, and she was guarding the prize.

"It's my bet the door isn't locked," I whispered to Danny. "They'll rely on the gate."

He nodded. I couldn't tell if that was good or bad.

We walked up to the house, opened the door, and went in.

I put my hand on Danny's arm to hold him back a minute. I was afraid the pounding of my heart would sound as subtle as jungle drums in that silent house. When the noise slacked off a little, we started forward toward the stairs.

The noise of my heart drowned out the sound of footsteps behind me. The guy had a good grip on my Adam's apple from behind before I even knew what was happening. Nobody made a sound. The guy wouldn't let go. I saw Danny's dark shape turning toward me. I gave up trying to move the guy's arm from my throat, and reached inside my jacket to the holster. That holster has served me well. It earned another polishing that night. My hand closed around the neck of the bottle and eased it out. My throat was starting to hurt from where the guy was inconsiderately squeezing it, so I swung the bottle behind me and smashed the heavy in the mouth.

He went down like a thousand-year-old redwood, muttering, "My teeth, my teeth," but I didn't care. I came around in a hurry and hit him again, hard. He stopped worrying about his teeth then.

The jungle drums were going again pretty good after that, but we started back up the stairs.

At the top, I looked down the corridor. A blade of light was coming from under one of the doors. It was Mary Cantrell's room.

We went in there like a pair of matched bullocks.

Mary was sitting on the edge of the bed. Standing over her was Elvira Hawkins, and she was smiling.

Danny and I couldn't even manage a grin.

Beside the bed was an intravenous stand and hanging from the top of it was a clear plastic I.V. bag. I saw some others on the night table. There was about a mile of plastic tubing, too, all stretched out and hooked up and ready to go. Elvira had one end of it in her hand, and attached to the tube was a hypodermic needle. She was bending over Mary's arm as she smiled, taking aim with that needle, and that's the way she froze, looking up at us.

For a while, everybody just looked things over, not saying anything. There wasn't much to say. I figured there were two possibilities. One was that the vampires were packing refreshments for a picnic, but I didn't like that one too much. The other was more terrible than I had time to think about just then.

I said, "Hello, Elvira."

Her smile turned real nasty and she snarled at me.

"We're onto your little game," I said, very polite and respectful, "but the game just came to an end."

She straightened up then. I couldn't tell if she was still snarling because Danny Lavender was wrapping one of his hands around her head.

Then Mary Cantrell was in my arms and I wasn't thinking about Elvira any more.

She sobbed for a while and kept turning those eyes up to me. I gave her all the time she needed to get herself calm again. Danny kept himself busy with Elvira.

After a while, I told Danny I thought we'd overstayed our welcome and maybe it was time we left. Elvira looked very subdued. Danny had her tied up securely with the plastic tubing.

"So long, sister," I said.

She mumbled something but I couldn't catch it. The gag in her mouth didn't improve her diction.

Mary was steady on her feet as we went down the stairs. She didn't need any coaxing to leave the house this time.

At the bottom of the stairs, the heavy we'd left there was starting to come around and maybe even remember his own name. I advised him to see a dentist, then hit him again with the bottle so he'd have to.

We didn't dawdle after that and got across the open patch okay and into the woods. It was a lot easier getting down the driveway than it had been hiking up. When we finally saw the car sitting there in the moonlight, with the trees politely standing aside for us to leave, I figured we were home free.

We piled into the front seat quick and got out of there.

I liked having Mary Cantrell safe on the seat beside me, and I liked having Danny Lavender protecting her on the other side.

About a mile down the road, I switched on the headlights and picked up some speed.

From behind me in the back seat, a voice said, "Do drive carefully, Mr. Kendall. We wouldn't want to have an accident now."

It happens like that sometimes. I'm the most suspicious person I know. I even know some credit managers who aren't as suspicious as I am. I always check the back seat of the car. I didn't check it that time.

Danny and I had never rehearsed it, but Dracula back there, in the person of Hawkins, he of the beauteous daughter, didn't have time to figure that out.

I swerved the car sharp to the left, then sharp to the right, then left again. Danny had had his arm across the back seat, behind Mary's shoulders, because otherwise his own shoulders wouldn't have let the three of us in the seat. While I was making the car imitate an eggbeater, Danny planted his elbow in the vampire's face.

I heard Mary Cantrell gasp beside me, but I didn't have time to think about that. I screeched the car to a stop and threw on the brake.

Danny was already climbing over the seat into the back and making sounds like he wasn't having a good time doing it. His compensation was that Drac wasn't having a good time, either. I joined him in the back as soon as the car stopped rocking.

He had the situation in hand already. I like a guy who thinks ahead and comes prepared for emergencies. Danny had kept half of that plastic tubing, and he was already getting Drac done up tight enough for special delivery.

"Put your finger there," Danny said, and pointed with his chin.

I put my finger there and held it till he pulled the last of the tubing tight.

"Okay," I said, and began to think maybe I'd take up breathing again.

"Look out!" Mary Cantrell cried.

I wished she'd been a little more precise, but in a second I figured out what was worrying her. The vampire was going for Danny Lavender's throat.

Danny snatched his head back just in time, but he continued leaning his arm against the vampire's chest.

"His teeth," Mary said. "You have to watch out for his teeth."

She was right.

Danny looked at me, without releasing his hold.

"Here," I said. I reached inside my jacket for the holster.

"Sorry I can't offer you a drink," I told Hawkins, showing him the bottle.

He said two words to me then that I don't want to write down. I used the back of my hand twice to make him regret each of them. After that he didn't say anything. It's not easy to talk with the neck of a booze bottle shoved down your throat and an angry Eskimo holding it in place.

4

After our little disagreement with Hawkins on the subject of neck-biting, we decided to sit out the rest of the night in the car and not risk driving while somebody held onto him.

We found a road down to the beach and parked there, waiting for daylight. If everything went according to Hoyle, the vampire was going to go into hibernation at dawn's early light.

Danny Lavender was in the back seat, nursing our friend with the bottle. Mary Cantrell stretched out across the front seat, saying she only needed to rest her eyes for a bit, and dozed off right away.

That left me.

I spend a lot of time thinking things over. It happens I have a lot of time in which to do that.

Now I was thinking about vampires, and I didn't like the thoughts I was having. In my business you get used to having new thoughts, learning new things, but sometimes you have to learn something you didn't really want to know. The worst of it was the fact that I'd already been believing in vampires and acting on that belief for most of the day. And the day had been pretty long.

In any prison, fellow cons will call a truce and gang up very cosily to erase a child molester or a traitor. I wondered what that fraternity would do to a vampire.

But then a vampire could never be put in a prison. That was going to be kind of a roadblock for me.

I listened to the ocean some more and wished I could slow my heartbeat down to its rhythm. I kept myself occupied by kicking some sand with the toe of my shoe. It didn't help my thinking any.

I knew I couldn't kill him. I've seen lots of murders and I know lots of interesting ways to go about it, but stakes through the heart just aren't in my line. I couldn't turn him over to the police. I couldn't kill him. I couldn't let him go. I had a real problem on my hands.

I kicked the sand some more but it just blew away on the breeze, like all my thoughts.

"I'm so sorry I got you involved in this," Mary Cantrell said softly at my side.

I turned my head and looked at her. People tell me I deal out the words pretty sharp, sometimes sharp enough to cut, but I didn't know what to be saying now. Also, I kept my hands in my pockets. If I'd taken them out, I might have been tempted to violate the client-investigator relationship. I looked at her, standing there in the silvery moonlight on the rippled sand of the beach, her skirt moving softly around her in the breeze from the ocean. She had her face tilted up to me. Those eyes. I looked away.

"I'll think of something," I said. I could hardly hear my own voice.

"I mean it," she said. She touched my arm with the tips of her fingers. "You're a good man, Mike Kendall. I can see that. You've already risked your life for me, and that's more than any fee can ever repay you for. I know you deal all the time with . . . with terrible people and the terrible things they do to each other. It must be awful, having to face that every day, having to face that knowledge. I've just learned something about that myself, so I understand a little of what you must feel."

I waved one hand to brush it all away. I didn't move the arm she was touching.

"This must be the worst thing you've ever had to deal with," she said. I could hear the sadness in her voice.

"I've seen worse," I said.

I hadn't.

I felt her hand tighten on my arm. I watched the ocean as if I expected Russian submarines to surface any minute. "I'll get us out of this," I told her. "I'll find a way."

"I know you will."

I spent some time trying to think of a way. I couldn't.

"Mike," she said. Just like that.

I turned to face her and we moved closer together. Nothing moved on the beach except the eternal ocean.

When we kissed, I could taste the salt on her lips.

Dawn can be beautiful in California, with the first pink light streaking up over the mountains, almost as beautiful as the red and gold and purple of sunset over the Pacific. This dawn wasn't beautiful at all. It was just gray and overcast and misty, but it was the best I'd ever seen.

The part of me that's mean wished I could take credit for solving the problem, but I couldn't. The problem solved itself.

About the time the first light began to touch the beach, the vampire in the back seat began making some unpleasant noises deep in his throat. He kept it up and after a while I heard Danny Lavender grunt. That wasn't a good sign, but if Danny had needed help, I would have known. Mary had gone back to sleep, stretched out like a child on the front seat of the car. I was still watching the ocean.

Then Hawkins started coughing as if he might choke, and I wondered if maybe Danny Lavender was forgetting his own strength. Besides, I was very attached to that particular bottle and I didn't want to lose it down the gullet of a vampire. I went back to see what was going on.

Hawkins had his eyes wide open and they were darting around in every direction, except he kept blinking madly, as if somebody were shining a spotlight into them. I thought he looked pretty pale, too. He was definitely not in the pink of health.

His tossing around and gurgling woke up Mary Cantrell, and the three of us studied him. I could see Mary's face filled with the most terrible sadness of all, the knowledge that someone you thought had loved you has now betrayed you.

Then something changed in the noises Hawkins was making. I wasn't expecting it from him so at first I didn't realize what it was. Then I caught it. There's a special kind of sound a man makes when he's gagged, not just the usual protests and faked noises of choking, but a sound that says clearly, if you've heard it before, that the subject has something to say and that maybe he's going to sing the song you want to hear. Danny Lavender was looking at me, waiting for a signal. He'd heard it, too.

"I think he wants to say something," Mary Cantrell said.

I looked at her and let my admiration show.

"Okay," I told Danny. "Uncork him."

Danny removed the bottle from the vampire's mouth, not taking too much care to avoid banging the bottle on his fangs. The vampire winced. I didn't like myself too much for it, but I enjoyed seeing that.

"You are all so foolish," were the vampire's first words.

The jungle drums started up again in my chest.

"So foolish," he said again, and started laughing. It was a weak laugh, but it was laughter. It made Mary Cantrell cry. I hit him for doing that.

His eyes glared at me, but the smile never left his face.

His voice was fading fast and his face was going more pale by the second. He was dying and suddenly we all knew it. But he was still smiling because he knew something else the rest of us didn't know.

Then he told us what he had to say and it was the worst thing I'd ever heard.

He told us everything, the whole ugly story. Nobody interrupted while he spoke. Dawn was getting brighter by the second, and he didn't have much time left.

"I want you to know this," he said. "Knowing that you have this knowledge will be the last and the greatest pleasure of my life.

"I know what happened in the bedroom upstairs. I know you left Elvira there, but rest assured that she has gotten herself free by now. She was always a resourceful girl. But she is not a vampire.

"You look surprised. No, she is not a vampire, nor are any of the other staff at Kirkdale, so you're safe on that score.

"It is true that I was planning to make them vampires, beginning with my dear Elvira, of course. And I was going to use your blood for that purpose, young lady. But that doesn't matter now. They will simply have to look out for themselves from now on in the lowly way of puny humans with limited human powers. And Elvira, I'm sure, will do well for herself. A good-looking girl can always do well in sunny California, eh?

"No, I was the only vampire at Kirkdale. And now I am dying. You have me and it seems obvious there is nothing I can do to escape. My powers are weakening. With every ray of dawning light that shines, I grow weaker. In minutes, I shall be dead."

His eyes were losing their gleam by the second, but as he looked at each of the three of us there was still a fierce light burning in them. And there was something else, too. There was amusement. I knew that with his last breath he was going to tell us something we didn't want to hear.

He looked at Danny Lavender a moment, then he looked at me, then he let his gaze come to rest on Mary Cantrell.

"I bit your father, young lady. Had you forgotten that? Oh, his blood tasted good. Quite rich and aristocratic and—"

"Stop it!" I said. "That's enough! You're having the last laugh anyway, so just get on with the story." I made a fist and showed it to him.

He smiled, but it looked as if it took almost the last bit of life left in him. He closed his eyes, then opened them again. He was still looking at Mary.

"Your father," he said. "I bit him. Now your father is a vampire!"

His eyes blazed for a second, but that was the end. California's vampire population went down by one.

The trouble was, California's vampire population had also gone up by one the day before.

Mary Cantrell's father was a vampire and we had to track him down before he killed others.

And if we found him, what were we going to do with him?

I didn't know. All I knew for sure right then was that Mary Cantrell was sobbing against my shoulder and I hated a world in which someone like her could be made to cry.

Pretty soon, the sun started doing ugly things to the vampire's body. Nobody said a word while we buried what was left. Then we got in the car and went away from that place.

5

We spent a little time going back up in the hills to the diner to get Danny's car and my own. They were still there. I hoped that might mean my luck was beginning to turn, but I knew better than to hope it too much.

Mary said she could drive her own car back to L.A. and my office. I let her. She needed some time by herself, but I could also see the set of her jaw and the old determination in her eyes. She'd had a bad night but she was going to be okay.

I told Danny Lavender to meet me at the office at dusk. I figured he'd be stirring again about the time Jonathan David Cantrell would be up and about. It was going to be a long day. But the day wasn't going to be as long as the next night.

Back at the office, I found Mary Cantrell sound asleep on the couch in my waiting room. That was more use than the couch had seen in years. It wasn't much but I was glad it was there for her. I reminded myself to dust it sometime. You never know when you're going to need a couch.

I locked the office when I left. I wanted to find Mary Cantrell there, safe and sound, when I got back.

My first stop was the local booze emporium. I wasn't taking any chances, so I bought a new bottle for my holster, plus another couple for good measure. It's a comforting feeling to know you're packing plenty of armament going into battle.

Then I went to Joe's Place and drank four cups of breakfast, black. I'm not usually an early type and Joe looked at me funny when I came in, but he knew enough to leave me alone and just keep the coffee coming.

I tried to think everything over again and figure where this road was leading us, but nothing made any sense till I started on the third cup. Coffee is important in my work. I think very highly of countries that grow it.

When Joe poured the fifth cup, he put a packet of Alka-Seltzer on the table beside the saucer. Joe is a good man.

I hated what I was thinking. I knew it was the only answer, the only way we were going to stop Jonathan David Cantrell, but I hated it anyway.

She was awake when I got there and one look at her face told me she'd figured it out, too. It didn't take a second look to tell me she was ready to go through with it.

"You know what has to be done," I said.

"Yes."

"I'm sorry."

"It can't be helped," she said. "I can do whatever I have to."

"You'll be risking your life. I wish there were some other way."

She shook her head. We both knew there wasn't.

Even a decent citizen who doesn't believe in vampires knows a lot about them. For one thing, they're creatures of habit, and that's the key to getting them. That was the first thing I'd realized, and that had led Mary and me to this conversation. I discounted all that stuff you hear about mirrors and garlic and dirt from the vampire's grave. Maybe it's true, maybe it's not. I didn't care. I only cared about what mattered most. And what mattered most and first was finding him.

In order to find him, we'd have to set a trap. But what do you lure a vampire with? Blood? Too easy. Everybody you pass on the street has blood. No, you have to use the one thing that pleases a vampire most, a chance to hurt the one person that vampire has most loved in life.

We were going to have to use Mary Cantrell herself as the bait to catch her own father.

That was pretty bad, about as bad as things can be. But there was still something else.

"I can't kill him," Mary said quietly. "And we can't just let him die, the way Hawkins did. I've already faced my father's death once. I can't face it again. We'll have to figure out something else."

"Yeah," I said. "I know. I just don't know what."

I didn't, either.

We didn't talk much during the day. Mary spent some time looking out the window, but it wasn't much nicer out than it was in. I kept myself busy studying the scars on my desk.

About one o'clock I had an idea.

"Tell me about your father," I said. "Tell me everything, whether you told it to me before or not. What I'm looking for is the things he cared most about. Besides you."

She started talking, telling me all sorts of things, the kinds of things that are awkward to talk about after somebody has died. Everything seems trivial in the light of the person's death. I listened carefully. I couldn't afford to think any of it was trivial, because somewhere in what Mary was telling me was the clue we needed.

I couldn't hear it. I listened, but I couldn't hear it.

"He had a lot of money," I said. "Did he give any of it away?"

"Yes," Mary told me. "He was very generous and supported a large number of charities."

"Who got the most?"

She thought about that. "There were all the usual charities," she said slowly, "but there was one that he was especially fond of. Yes, I think they may have gotten even more than the others."

I waited.

"It was the zoo."

"The zoo?" I said.

"The zoo in Santa Bonita. It was only a small zoo for many years, and of course overshadowed by the San Diego Zoo. But the group of directors there wanted to expand it. I don't know if they went to my father or if he first approached them, but I know he gave them a lot of money in recent years." She looked at me. "A lot of money. He loved animals almost as much as he loved flowers. I'm sorry I forgot to mention that before."

"It's okay," I said. "We've got it now. Or half of it, anyway." I stood up. "Let's take a ride."

"Where are we going?"

"The zoo," I told her.

We got there just before closing time, and the guard at the gate didn't want to let us in. Mary asked him to call the head office and tell them she was there. I don't know if it was her voice or her eyes that got him to make the call. He was back in less than a minute, and in two minutes more that guard was riding us around on his motor cart, showing us all the sights.

I was looking for something, but I wouldn't know what it was until I spotted it.

After about fifteen minutes, we'd seen everything there was to see but I still hadn't seen what I was looking for.

"Let's go around again," I told the guard. He was pretty cheerful about cooperating. Overtime is good money.

We went a little distance and then I told him to stop.

"What's that?" I asked him.

He glanced over where I was pointing. "Not finished yet," he said.

I put my hand on his shoulder. He looked at me and I let him read my face.

"Oh," he said. "You asked me what it is, didn't you? Right. Well, in about a week's time, it's going to be the new World of Night exhibit."

I didn't want to look at Mary Cantrell.

"Tell me about it," I said.

"Well, you remember how they used to have, you know, the snake house and the rodent exhibit and like that? But it didn't work out so good because all those things sleep all day long and only go out hunting for food at night. Kind of like the graveyard shift of the animal kingdom. . . . Do you get it?"

I looked at him some more.

"Right," he said. "So in a World of Night exhibit, what they do is, they turn around day and night by putting all the lights on a different schedule. Fools the animals, see? When people are here in the day-time, it's dark inside, kind of like moonlight, but the animals think it's nighttime and they're all up and going about their business. Then at night, real night, when there's nobody in the zoo to see them, the lights are on in the exhibit and the animals all go to sleep. Works out fine."

"When is it supposed to open?"

"Next week. Everything is done except the finishing touches. And, of course, they have to bring the animals in. They'll start doing that tomorrow."

"What's it called?" I asked him.

"I told you that. The World of Night."

"Any other name?"

"Oh, you mean like a benefactor? Yeah, some guy gave a few million bucks to build it and they put his name on it to be official. Boy, some people just don't know what to be doing with their money. Building a new home for a bunch of rats and snakes. Boy!"

"Yeah," I said. "I know how you feel. Ain't it something?"

"Yeah," he said.

"Yeah. Listen, the lady here needs a private room with a telephone."

"Oh, sure," he said right away, and I could tell from the look on his face that he was suddenly remembering what the front office had told him about showing this particular lady around.

"Yep, some people with money are real generous, you know that?" he said.

"I know," I said. "The telephone?"

"Right over there in the main office. I'll show you the way."

"You know what I'm thinking," I said to Mary Cantrell when we were alone.

She looked at me. She knew.

I called Danny Lavender first and told him to meet us there as soon as possible.

I didn't have to tell Mary who to call.

She got the chairman of the board of directors on the phone and told him what we needed. She also told him that if anything ever went wrong or if a word of this ever leaked out, that zoo would never see another cent of Cantrell money. On the other hand, if everything went well, she thought that perhaps in a couple of years it might be time to expand the zoo's facilities further. She also allowed as how she was very pleased with the work he was doing himself, and that work as good as his deserved to be rewarded.

Money talks. It just talks a different language from the one I learned as a child. I listened to it the way I'd listen to somebody talking French.

Mary Cantrell was terrific. She didn't even have trouble reassuring the chairman that her father was quite well but out of town for an extended period.

She put the chairman on hold, went to the door, and called in the security guard. He put the phone to his ear and listened for a few minutes and said, "Yes, sir," a few times.

When he put the phone down again, he looked very respectful.

"I'll have the keys to the World of Night for you right away," he said, and went out of there like a shot.

I thought it would break my heart to see that brave little girl sitting out there on that stone wall by herself in the darkness. She just sat there, waiting, her eyes searching all around. I felt like an oaf, clumsy and helpless. I knew from the angle of his head that Danny Lavender felt the same way. We were about a hundred feet away from her on each side. We waited. That's all we could do.

I kept thinking what a long shot it was. Maybe he wouldn't come here at all. Maybe he was off in some other place right now, sucking somebody's blood. Maybe he was, but I couldn't think about that now. We were betting he'd come here and we were using his daughter's life to bet with and I had to concentrate on that.

And then I saw him.

I was looking at the second vampire I'd ever seen. That's a lot of vampires when you didn't even believe in them thirty-six hours before. You learn quick in this business to keep an open mind.

He was stalking her. I can't describe it any other way.

She saw him about the same time I did. I looked over to where Danny was hiding but I couldn't see him. I wished I could, I would have felt better, but I figured he was up to something and that was okay.

I looked back at the vampire. He was standing behind a tree, watching her. Then he moved forward, to another tree. It was dark, but I thought I saw his shoulders shaking. He was laughing. He was laughing because he was going to wreak the ultimate damage on the very person he most loved.

I thought about the ironies of life for a second. Then there was no more time to think because the vampire was moving closer to Mary again.

I wished I knew where Danny Lavender was.

Danny and I had tried to work out a plan as soon as he'd met us there. I've mixed it up with the best of them—that is to say, the worst—and so has Danny, but we couldn't figure out how to handle this case. Clobber him, was the best I could come up with. My holster was loaded and Danny had his fists. We had no other weapons. Besides, anything else we might have used would have been about as useful as hair on a golf ball. We were going to play it as it came, and never mind the risks. Anyway, Mary Cantrell was taking the biggest risk of all.

I watched the vampire moving closer to her. The jungle drums were going a mile a minute.

There was still no sign of Danny. I kept wishing I knew where he was.

Then Mary Cantrell was standing up to face her father.

"Hello, Daddy," she said. Her voice sounded steady.

He laughed, right out loud, gloating.

"I know what you want from me, Daddy, but—"

Now he threw his head back in the moonlight and laughed at the night like a jackal. It was the worst sound I'd ever heard. The moonlight shone on his fangs. He started reaching for her.

I stepped out from hiding.

"Hey!" I shouted.

He swung around, distracted for what turned out to be a crucial second. He snarled and took a step toward me. I was glad to see Mary move backwards, away from him.

I didn't know exactly what I was going to do, but I went toward him anyway.

"Got the time?" I said.

He threw his head back again to laugh but the laugh was cut off short. We found out at the same time where Danny Lavender had been.

In that same second, the vampire turned even whiter than he'd been to start with and spun around in confusion, momentarily off balance. That moment was just enough for me to race across the pathway and caress the back of his head a couple of times with my favorite weapon. The vampire didn't go out completely, but he went down for the count without further protest.

I wasn't surprised that even the vampire was frightened for a second. I'd be willing to bet that anybody would be pretty frightened if nearly three hundred pounds of albino Eskimo suddenly dropped from a branch above him, naked in the moonlight except for his white cotton Fruit of the Looms, and yelling at the top of his voice some Eskimo words that he probably didn't learn at his mother's knee.

We didn't waste any time. Danny grabbed for the vampire's arms and I picked up his feet and we ran for the back door of the World of Night. Mary had kept her head through it all and had the door open wide for us.

We didn't have to carry him very far to the room we'd picked out, but I thought we'd never get there in time. I kept looking at those fangs.

Then we had him inside.

"Kiss the vampire goodbye," I told Mary Cantrell.

She did. On the forehead.

For her sake, I would have liked to put him down a little more gently, but there wasn't time for that. We dumped him and got out of there and locked the door behind us.

Mary slept on the couch in my waiting room that night. I slept with my face on the desk. The scars were rough to sleep on but none of that mattered.

When I woke up, Mary Cantrell was standing in front of the desk.

All she said was, "Thank you."

I waved a hand.

We went across to Joe's Place. Joe took one quick look at her and was very impressed.

"I just pray that it's a permanent solution," she said quietly after a while.

"It's as permanent as we can make it," I told her. "The Cantrell Foundation will endow the World of Night in perpetuity, with a provision that no changes can be made in the building without the Foundation's approval. Except for the new wall sealing off that room and a slight rearrangement inside the building. And if he ever does get out, it'll be in the daylight."

"Yes," she said. There was nothing else to say.

We went back to my office for a minute and she got out her checkbook and wrote me a check.

Then I saw her to the door and silently declared the case closed.

When I looked at the check, I saw it was for more than my fee. I split the difference with Danny Lavender. I owed him a lot.

That was the last I ever heard of Mary Cantrell, except for a note I had from her a few weeks later. She told me she had fixed things with the lawyers and her father was now officially deceased. The servants had all decamped for parts unknown, and now she was alone in the world. She was taking the money she inherited and going away someplace to start a new life where nothing would ever remind her of the past. I never saw her again.

The city is a jungle and I live in it every day, and like the real jungle, it's filled with wild beasts. But unlike those beasts, I have a memory. I know that Mary Cantrell is safe now and I know that she kissed me that night on the beach with the moonlight shining on her hair.

I must write myself a note to remember that sometime, to think about it. It'll be like a vacation. It'll be nice.

The Man Who Killed Forever

Prologue

The hero of this story is a man named Clayton Bannister and you need to know some things about him right from the start.

I've told some other yarns before this, and if the Lord is willing, I reckon I'll live to tell some more—I know some good ones I haven't put down on paper yet—but this one I'm starting here happened to people I was acquainted with myself, so I guess I know what's required.

Clayton Bannister didn't hold with lying, though he'd told a few good ones in his time. He didn't hold with going back on a deal or a promise, whether it was written down proper or only spoken out on a handshake, but he'd broken his word too sometimes. He didn't hold with being a coward but he'd felt that cold sweat on his back and he'd done some running when it fit the circumstances. He didn't hold with murder, but at the time I'm telling about he'd killed fourteen men and two women, and none of them died accidental deaths.

In years after, among the folks who knew him, he came to be known as The Man Who Killed Forever.

This is the story of how he did it.

1

He was in a town called Two Trails, which was right on the western edge of the desert and at the eastern edge of the mountains. It was a small town, the way they were in those parts in those days, but it was a decent sort of place, filled with decent folks, mostly. It only had the one main street right down the middle, with stores and a couple of saloons and a couple of harness and blacksmith shops and so on and the Elite Hotel and Restaurant right in the middle looking pretty grand for a town that size. There was a white church at the eastern end of the street which was kind of nice-looking too and only a little smaller than the Elite.

Funny thing about the name of that town: Two Trails. East of it, across the desert, there was a dusty track hardly fit to be called a road. That track started out far away in the east and then led straight as a rifle shot into the end of town where that church was standing. It continued on straight ahead with the stores and saloons on either side for a stretch, and then headed on out the west side of town, still running just as straight as ever, and climbed up into the foothills and then higher up into the mountains themselves.

It was just that one solitary road. But it really was two trails, if you look at it right. There was that road pointing back east, to Independence or Kansas City and places like that, where everybody in that town had come from in the beginning, more or less. And there, on the other side of town, was that road pointing on into the west, toward those mountains, and somewhere on the other side of those mountains was California.

If you had a good horse—and if you bought it from Fred Mitchum, who had the biggest spread in those parts, it was a good one—and you rode it half a day's ride from Two Trails, you could be in wild desert country, nothing but switchbacks and rocky creekbeds and twisted mesquite or else windy, stony hills with pretty uncertain footing for man or horse. If you rode that horse for a full day, you could have your brains baking like pan bread in the desert sun or your blood freezing solid in the mountains. Two Trails was a good name for that place, all right.

I guess it's a good thing to be reminded of, that every road a man might stand on points in two directions at once. Which road it is depends on the man and what he's looking for, is all.

In part, that's what this story is about, I guess.

Two Trails had just about enough good grazing land in the surrounding area to support Fred Mitchum's big horse ranch and two medium-size cattle spreads, and then there were a few small farms as well closer in to town. Heavy goods for the shops came mostly by mule train from the East—tools and hardware and such—but otherwise that town didn't need much from outside. It could keep itself pretty well supplied with horses and beef and vegetables and flour—

man named Martin Raines had a little flour mill he built with his own two hands, and two donkeys to run it that he treated better than some folks treat their children—and so in consequence Two Trails always kept pretty much to itself.

That's why Clayton Bannister went there.

He wasn't a youngster anymore at that time, and he wasn't old, either, but just about the age a man begins to see he's not going to live forever. You reach that age and then you see it, see that you're going to have to die just like everybody else sooner or later, really see it, and all of a sudden you want to stop what you're doing and think some on that point. Some men do, anyway. Leastways, Clayton Bannister did.

He'd been around some before that, seen different places, worked different jobs. Something inside him kept him from staying too long in one place, always had him looking for something else after a while. True, he never minded working for another man when the mood was on him, but he always needed to feel that he was still in charge of himself, that he could up and say anytime he wanted, no thank you, I'll be moving on now.

He'd hired on at cattle ranches and horse ranches and lived in the saddle and slept on the ground for weeks and months at a time, all over the West. He'd worked at guarding a bank's money too and kept regular hours and lived in a proper room like a civilized man. He'd spent a year riding on the high box of a Concord with a heavy shotgun across his knees and a good Spencer rifle at his side and a sturdy Colt near his hand, guarding freight and gold and passengers, looking out at the land and watching the line of the horizon. He liked that, sitting up there on the Concord, seeing the land and the sky and watching the colors change and the shadows move as time passed from dawn till sunset. Sometimes there was a little skirmish, maybe Indians, maybe gunfighters. He never lost anything he was asked to protect. Well, he did that particular job for a year or so, and then he got to know that stretch of land along the stage route so well that if a gopher changed its burrow and started in to raising a family he knew it the same day, and then it was time for him to move on, same as he'd always done before.

A man with the inclination to think has plenty of time to do it in the West. There's all the sky and all the silence and all the shadows sliding slow and steady across all those empty miles. So when Clayton Bannister got to thinking he'd have to die one day, same as he'd seen so many other fellows die, he figured the time had come for him to think that through and make his peace with it.

He wanted to go someplace he'd never been before. Mostly, he would have liked to go someplace where nobody'd know who he was, but he'd killed a number of men famous in the West already for their misdeeds and that made him a little bit famous too. Funny thing how a man can be famous for killing and not be a killer himself.

But that was the case and he reckoned that his reputation preceded him most places he might go, so he might just as well bear with it and go wherever he wanted. He'd give another name, he figured, to anyone who asked, and if he was lucky there'd be nobody in the region who'd recognize his face. John Nelson was the name he decided on, nice and simple and easy to forget, a name you might have heard before and might not. But there was no way he could disguise the width of his shoulders or the height of his stature or the way he carried himself, the way a man does who owes answers to nobody on this earth. Well, he'd just have to trust to luck for that.

He was never much given to buying things other than essentials—never saw many things he wanted besides the freedom to move on—so he had a stake that would last him a pretty long while. He had enough, in fact, to let him settle a little piece of land and then prove up and own it outright in five years' time, but he didn't know if he really wanted to do that. Maybe possessing the land and just having it are different things, and he already had it, as much as he wanted.

Well, Two Trails sounded mighty good to him, from what he'd heard of it. Nice little town, decent folks mostly, and just that one road passing through the middle, sort of daring a man in a quiet sort of way to make up his mind where he was headed. Clayton Bannister liked the look of it.

And there was one other thing too about that town. It was farther west than he had ever been before. Something was drawing him there, maybe a whim, maybe destiny, but he felt the call and he felt the need to answer it.

So off he headed for Two Trails. He had money in his pocket, his Colt and his Winchester, the good horse he was riding and the clothes on his back, and there was noplace he had to be by any particular time for the rest of his life.

He thought he'd have some quiet times in Two Trails.

What he got instead was the worst thing he'd ever had to face, before then or after. It makes the back of my neck prickle even today just to think about it.

2

So there he was in Two Trails, living in a room he rented in a farmhouse, paying his rent regular every week and keeping pretty much to himself. There were folks in town who knew who he was, all right, but he was a quiet-keeping man, hard to talk to and impossible to get anything out of, so mostly everyone left him alone.

He had just finished eating his noonday meal one Saturday at the Elite Hotel and Restaurant—they served good food there, plain and plenty of it—and stepped outside to sit a spell and pass the time of day on the sidewalk in a kind of mutual silence with Old Jed Tree.

Old Jed claimed to be more than a hundred years old. Maybe he was. He claimed a lot more besides that, but no one in Two Trails put much stock in any of it. Jed loved to tell tales about his heroic exploits as a young man. There was one about how he'd crawled across the blazing desert on his hands and knees, burning up by day and shivering by night, for three days and three nights. Which was the cause of his current lumbago, if you believed the story at all. There was a tale about him swimming across the rampaging Colorado River when an ox lost courage and drowned underneath him. And there was another one about how he lived three years with the Arapaho and wore out every wife they gave him. They were good stories, mostly, and Old Jed was a free show, so people generally listened and nodded and then went on about their business.

But when it came to finding out anything you needed to know about Two Trails or anyone in it, dead or alive, or gossip about your neighbors, or word about who might be rustling some other fellow's wife, everybody in that town turned to Old Jed first.

The important thing, I guess, was that Old Jed had a knack for hearing things and gathering news, and most of his knack came from the fact that he had greater endurance, despite the years piling up on him, than anyone else in that town. When he wasn't telling his own tales, he listened and let everybody else talk. No one knew where his money came from, but he always had the price of his meals and his room at Mrs. Campbell's boardinghouse. He could stand up in the sun, too, if he wanted, prouder than any unbroken stallion, and stand there till everybody else had fallen over with the heatstroke. And he could walk a longer distance, too, than some horses people had paid a lot of good money to buy. You wouldn't have thought it to look at him, with that grizzled beard and those broken, yellow teeth and that stoop in his shoulders, but he could do all of that and a powerful lot more besides.

So there he was, that Saturday afternoon, sitting on a straight chair on the sidewalk outside the Elite Hotel and Restaurant, just sitting in the shade, leaning on the head of his cane, an old man lazing through the day and waiting for sunset, and Clayton Bannister sitting there beside him, neither one of them saying a word.

It was Saturday, a little after noon, and folks had come in from all around to do a little business or shopping or just plain resting up. The road and the sidewalks on either side of it were pretty crowded. Some of the young ones were running and yelling the way they like to do and most of the women had shopping baskets on their arms.

Clayton Bannister was sitting out there beside Jed, just sort of keeping him silent company and looking at people passing by and thinking his own thoughts, when Old Jed cleared his throat in that meaningful way he did sometimes. He'd do it just before he said something he wanted you to pay special attention to.

"Here he comes," he said. He said it real flat and quiet and he didn't say another word else. Just that: "Here he comes."

Clayton Bannister moved his eyes and looked where Old Jed was looking.

A lot of other folks were looking too.

It was like a slow wind was moving down that street, pushing people out of the road and back against the walls. It was like maybe part of the sun had started burning real fierce all of a sudden and a wall of heat was moving east through the town and the only thing you could do was give way and back off.

A rider dressed all in black, on a tall black horse, was coming along the middle of the road, real slow. As he passed, people on both sides dropped whatever they were doing or saying and turned around to look at him. He passed some horses hitched outside Feeley's and a couple of them nickered and shied away, real skittish behavior for town horses. That rider paid no mind to any of it, not turning his head left or right. He just kept coming, moving real slow and looking real big on that tall horse, with the road emptying behind him and the people in the streets looking out from the shade on both sides.

Dust rose up in a yellow cloud behind that horse, but even in the hot, still air, it seemed to just hurry away behind him and go lay down real quiet someplace else, as if it feared to get out in front of that man or even stay too close.

"Looks like a ha'nt," said Old Jed, real quiet like before.

He was something to see, that stranger.

He was big, tall, sitting straight in the saddle, shoulders looking as broad as the horse beneath him and with a head of a size to match. He was turned out real handsome, too, every bit of his clothes and kit just as black as the horse he was riding. Black boots, trousers, belt, holster, shirt, neckerchief, hat, and a black gun butt sticking up straight and prominent at his hip and a black rifle stock riding by his leg. He held black reins in black-gloved hands, resting easy on the pommel. His saddle and bedroll and those bulging saddlebags behind him were black too, gleaming in the sun just like the horse and his boots. They were fairly shining, not a speck of trail dust or sweat on man or horse, not a sign of the long, lonely road that's the only way into or out of Two Trails.

You couldn't see anything of his face, with the wide brim of his hat bent down in front and hiding it from the sun, making a shadow like the edge of a knife across his chest, but you knew without thinking what those eyes would be like. They'd be black too, deep and dark like a quarry pool in the farthest back corner of hell. And maybe you couldn't tell right off what eyes like that might be looking for, but you knew they'd look and look hard and not stop looking till they found it.

Funny thing, how a picture like that can remind you for a second of maybe a dog or a wolf. Some wild animals, they give that appearance, like they've seen everything, the great cities of Europe, all that stuff from the ancient world and all the rest of it, and none of it impresses them. They don't need it. They just have themselves, wild creatures like that, and they have a purpose, and not a thing else in the world makes any kind of consequence to them.

No question about it, that rider meant trouble, the blackest sort of trouble, riding into town. Everybody there felt it as sure as they felt the burning heat of the sun.

Clayton Bannister watched him same as everybody else, not saying a word. He felt something down deep in his insides turn hard and still, almost painful. And something back in a corner of his mind told him something he didn't want to know. He knew that feeling. It was something he'd felt more than once before and it had told him the truth every time. Now it was telling him this was a man he was going to have to kill one day.

That was the first time he laid eyes on the man who called himself Forever.

It wasn't twenty minutes after that before the shooting started and five good men were dead.

3

You couldn't see his hands move but that stranger drew rein right in front of the Elite and turned the horse to face the front doors. People were gathering to watch on the sidewalk on both sides of the road. It got real quiet real quick there in the middle of town and a few fellows drifted out from the Elite's saloon to see what all the silence was about. Their boots made a loud thumping and scraping sound on the wooden planks. The stranger just sat there on that black horse, looking at the hotel. For a long spell, nobody said a word.

One of the fellows from the Elite saloon put his head back inside and called out, but kind of low, "Hey, Tom, here's some business for you, if you want it."

Then after a minute Tom Pinkwater, who was owner and proprietor of the Elite Hotel and Restaurant, came sauntering out through the batwing doors. He was a kind of round-faced, pink-faced kind of fellow and he was squinting at the sunlight and still drying a glass on the corner of his apron.

Some more fellows followed him outside, always eager to see a curiosity, and more boots thumped and shuffled on the sidewalk and a pair of spurs made a jingling noise.

"It's some kinda sideshow magician," one of the men said with a sneer, but there might have been some nervousness deep down in his voice too. A couple of the men snorted and nodded in approval and one poked another with his elbow, but most of the others didn't say a thing.

For a while there, it was as quiet as probably it's ever been in Two Trails. It seemed like everybody was holding their breath, just looking at that fellow on the horse where he kind of made a big black hole in the sunlight.

"Who's in charge here?" said the rider all in black, but he made it sound like he knew already. He spoke real quiet but his voice filled the empty street and every man standing there on the sidewalk could hear him plain as day.

There was some shuffling around in front of the Elite. In the middle of it Clayton Bannister stood up but he did it behind some other men where the stranger couldn't see him. Somebody gave Tom Pinkwater a shove in the ribs and he stepped forward to the edge of the sidewalk. His boots thumped loudly on the wood.

"Hotel's intended for strangers," Tom said, real low, to the fellows around him, "but that's the strangest one I ever seen."

Then he left off drying the glass and straightened himself up.

"I am," he called out. "That is, if it's a room and a meal you're after. I own the hotel."

For a long time, the stranger didn't move. The horse under him didn't move either, not even switching his tail or flicking an ear at the flies.

Then at last he said, "I have business with you."

And he just sat there, waiting, ignoring the burning sun.

Tom Pinkwater called back, "What kind of business? Come in out of the sun and we'll talk about it."

That stranger didn't move a muscle.

"Well, all right, then, what do you want?" Tom called back.

"What's your price?" the stranger said.

"Dollar a night," Tom answered up real quick, figuring this was something regular he could deal with.

When the stranger made no reply, Tom added, "Meals and drinks extra."

The stranger said nothing.

Nobody was moving, and there was just the weight of the sun pouring down.

"I might be able to fix up a weekly rate," Tom went on. Everybody could hear he was talking just a little too fast. "Or monthly, maybe, if you're fixing on staying a while. Depends."

There was still no reply from the stranger.

"You're on your own for the rest," Tom said.

Men who'd ridden hard and alone for a long time needed more than a roof and a meal and a bottle of liquor at the end of the trail before they felt whole again. The stranger didn't look like he'd ridden but the length of the street, maybe, but he must have come a far distance. Every place else in the world is a far distance from Two Trails.

"The hotel," the stranger said, in that same flat tone as before. "How much do you want for it?"

And then he just sat there and waited, with all the time in the world, for Tom's answer.

Tom shifted his weight from one leg to the other. You could tell that he was thinking the same thing other folks there were thinking. That stranger wasn't just having fun with him. That stranger meant exactly what he said.

A couple of the men standing there glanced sideways at Tom but then looked back to watch the stranger. He was more interesting. Across the road, some folks were edging out so they could hear better what was going on.

In front of the Elite, Clayton Bannister was watching everything. His eyes were narrowed to slits against the sun and his jaw looked set pretty hard.

"He's having you on, Tom," somebody whispered.

"Shut up," someone else said.

Tom answered after a minute. "Not for sale," he said, but a lot of men there would have been willing to bet he didn't even sound convincing to himself.

The rider in black said nothing. Slowly the white dust settled back to the road. The sun was blinding and the heat was enough to make a weary man start taking shorter breaths. That stranger was prepared to sit out there in the blazing sun and wait forever.

Tom Pinkwater shifted his weight again. His boots scraping on the dry wood made the only sound in the street. He cleared his throat, stalling for time. Plenty of folks in Two Trails could have figured rightly they knew everything that was going through his mind just then.

Like most everybody else in Two Trails, Tom Pinkwater loved the place and hated it, the sun, the dust, the distance from everywhere else in the world, the loneliness, the baking desert in the east that he'd crossed and the freezing mountains in the west that had blocked his path. This was as far as he'd gotten on the westward road, and now he'd been here so long, it felt almost like home some of the time.

And everybody there knew what that Elite Hotel and Restaurant meant to Tom too. Here was a man who'd set out for California, left the East behind and headed west, carrying in his pockets and on his back and in a single dusty wagon everything he owned and everything he ever hoped to be. He was going to make it all the way across, he'd read all those pamphlets about the wonders of California and about how all you had to do was drop a seed in the ground and then jump back out of the way, or set up your office or your shop and the money would come rolling in in no time at all and there was always a cool breeze to make you comfortable while you counted it. But by the time he'd reached this little settlement in the valley, the road had already grown too hot and hard and dry, and Tom Pinkwater knew that from here on out it gets steep and bitter cold besides. It was too much. He stayed where he was, and added another to the population of Two Trails.

The wagon trains used to pass along that road in great numbers and they still came from time to time then. They'd camp for a day or a week just outside the town and the merchants of Two Trails sold them mostly food and some equipment and tools and then they moved on out toward the mountains and the west and the people of Two Trails stayed where they were and watched them go. And most trains that passed through left one or two people behind, maybe a woman who'd lost her husband or a man who'd lost what was inside him to begin with back in Kansas City, something valuable that got ground into the dust between there and here and the loss of which kept him from going any farther.

Tom Pinkwater was like that. You could see it in his eyes.

Now he'd made something new for himself. He had the Elite. It was a good business and he was an honest businessman and that hotel was his life. It meant everything to him. He'd been intending to set up a hotel in California for all the rich folks out there and so become a rich man himself. He'd brought some pretty rosewood furniture with him from back East, all the way from Boston, Massachusetts, and he'd fixed up the Elite real nice and he served good food and everybody liked him and the town meetings, when the town bothered to hold them, which wasn't very often, were held in his dining room, and Tom Pinkwater, deep down in the private-most part of himself, hated every board and nail in the Elite worse than he'd ever hated anything else in his life and hoped never to hate as long as he lived.

"Not for sale," he said again, but he said it so low it was a wonder his voice carried all the way out to the stranger.

The rider shifted the angle of his head a little and the movement made it look like his whole body was laughing at Tom.

"Just you name it," he said, in that same hard voice.

That's how it is sometimes. Fellow puts a simple business proposition to you and the rest of your life depends on it.

Tom looked back at the stranger and took a deep breath. He closed his eyes for just a second, like a little child making a wish too precious to be let out in the light of day, and then he looked straight at the rider all in black and raised up his chin. And then he called out a price that was so amazingly high that a few of the men around him let out a sharp breath or muttered something without even knowing they did it.

"Half," the stranger said.

Tom Pinkwater let out a long, slow breath and went back to polishing that glass on his apron. "Then it's as I said," he called out. "Not for sale." He started to turn away, then stopped and looked back at the stranger. "You want a room or a meal, I got both available." Then he continued on his way and went right back inside that hotel.

Some of the men went inside with him and after a few seconds the crowd on both sides of the street began to drift away a little now that the show was over.

The stranger moved his horse forward to the steps. He left the reins hooked over the pommel and then, so quick and easy you could hardly see him do it, he dismounted. He moved like maybe a mountain lion running downhill or the shadow of an owl in the night. He went up the two wooden steps, crossed the sidewalk, and followed Tom Pinkwater inside. He didn't look left nor right when he did it. Without seeming to hurry, he moved so fast and smooth and easy that no one standing there even got a good look at his face.

Clayton Bannister followed the others inside and Old Jed Tree came creaking to his feet and followed along too.

The stranger had taken a seat in the dining room. Everybody else was settling themselves back to normal, starting in to resume their conversations, but you could tell they were all keeping an eye on the newcomer.

"What'll it be?" Tom Pinkwater said from behind the bar.

"Bottle of whiskey and a hot meal," the stranger said. His hat was still on his head and his face was still hidden. He was still wearing the black gloves.

Tom delivered the bottle and a shot glass to the table, then went back behind the bar. Some more people drifted in. The sheriff, Emmett Bridges, was one of them, making a show of looking real casual, but everybody knew right off that he'd heard about the stranger and the look of trouble on him, and he figured his services might be required. Two of the town's three deputies, Will Ash and Sam Frederickson, were with him. After a while, Andy Benjamin came in too. He was the other deputy, so now they were all there in the room with the stranger, along with a lot of other folks who wouldn't ordinarily have shown up at the Elite for another couple hours yet.

Nothing happened for a while, just people talking and drinking and playing a few friendly games of cards. The stranger worked on that bottle, doing some serious damage to its contents.

Clayton Bannister was over near the front door, just leaning back against the wall, watching the stranger. Funny how a big man like that can just kind of fade into the background like a shadow when he wants to.

When Tom brought over the stranger's meal, the man raised his head and said, "I'd appreciate somebody taking my horse to the livery stable."

Tom said he'd arrange it and looked around for a youngster to send on the errand. His eye fell on young Billy Wagner's towhead. Billy had edged close to get a good look at the stranger. Now he tried to slip away but Tom looked right at him and said, "Billy, you take care of that."

Young Billy slid away and in about a second or so he collared another youngster, then dug in his pocket for a coin. He handed over the coin and the other young fellow dashed out to see about the horse. Billy started edging his way back around the wall of the Elite so he wouldn't miss anything.

That was interesting, as things turned out, because young Billy was just about the only person in Two Trails that Clayton Bannister —or John Nelson, as folks there knew him—had spent any time talking to since he'd come to town. Young Billy and Old Jed Tree, that is, were the only two. Billy was an orphan, and since his folks died he'd spent his time moving around that town, living with each family in turn, earning his keep by doing odd jobs, the way he wanted, so in a way you could say that boy belonged to everybody and to nobody at the same time. In that way maybe he was a little like Old Jed, and maybe that's what Clayton Bannister liked about the two of them.

By the time Billy was back in his place, the stranger had started talking to Tom Pinkwater and you could feel the room growing quiet.

"Nice place," the stranger said. He sounded friendly, almost. "Real nice."

"I think so," Tom said, real cautious.

"Very thing I'm looking for," the stranger said. He hadn't touched the food. It was good food too. "You might say it was *exactly* the thing I'm looking for."

"What's that?" Tom said, but you could tell he knew.

"This hotel. I'm buying it."

Tom stared down at him and looked real sad.

"Now listen here, stranger," he said. "I run a clean and peaceable hotel, and I'd be mighty pleased to rent you a room and sell you a meal for as long as you care to stay. I'd even be pleased to buy you those drinks you're drinking, as a kind of welcome gesture. But I told you before. The hotel just ain't for sale." And he put his hands on his hips to kind of emphasize what he was saying.

The stranger lifted his glass one more time and drained it dry. Then he reached under his chair. More than a few of the men present let their right hands drop down in the vicinity of their guns when he did that, but it wasn't a gun he brought up. It was those black saddlebags. Nobody'd even seen him pull them off the horse outside, he'd moved so quick and easy, but there they were.

Without speaking a word, he reached inside one of those bags and brought out a handful of gold coins and tossed them on the table.

They made a loud noise and some of them rolled onto the floor and spun a bit before they lay down. But before they'd even stopped rolling, the stranger was doing the same with another handful, and another and another. The sound those coins made was the only sound in the Elite because nobody there was moving and hardly anybody was even breathing.

Like everybody else, Tom Pinkwater couldn't say a word. He just stared at all that gold.

"Enough?" the stranger said, and you could tell he was sneering.

Tom Pinkwater was going through a kind of agony. Every muscle in his body wanted to bend down and scoop up that gold. And yet there was a pride in the man that kept him from bending, kept him from being forced. After a minute, he managed to raise his head a little and look that stranger in the face.

"No," he said. "You don't have enough here and you never will."

Everybody in that room let out a breath at the same time.

"See here, my friend," the stranger said, and it was chilling to hear him use that word. "Let me tell you a story and see if you recognize in it anybody you know. There was this fellow, see, who came out to the West. You know the type, a fellow figuring on making a big fortune. Figuring on opening a fancy hotel, see, to cater to all the fancy folks and swells. He had a little stake too, not a lot, but some. But what he was really lacking was the heart for it, the courage, the nerve. He got partway to where he was going and then he lost the little nerve he had, so he just sat down right where he was. Now, friend, if that man was standing right here in front of me the way you are now, do you know what I'd tell him? Why, I'd tell him to take his yellow hide right back where he came from to Boston, Massachusetts. I'd tell him to take what was offered to him and go back there and maybe open a little rooming house on some quiet little street where he can live out his days in peace and won't nobody know him for the yellow coward he is."

And he poured himself another drink of Tom Pinkwater's liquor and drank it down in one swallow.

Not a man in that room but wasn't sweating. Some still had their hands resting light on their guns, but even so.

And then Tom Pinkwater did it. He just sank down to the floor like his knees couldn't hold him up. He had tears in his eyes and he murmured something real low, and then he began scooping up those gold coins like a blind man that can't hardly see what he's doing.

Well, that was too much.

Sheriff Emmett Bridges stepped forward from the crowd near the bar. He was plenty nervous, not understanding what was going on but knowing it wasn't right. He was a good man, Emmett Bridges, and he'd been keeping Two Trails peaceable for nearly eight years. Most troublemakers took one glance at the hard look in his eye and the determined jut of his jaw and decided it was time to move on.

"I think that's enough, stranger," he said. "I think you've made too much trouble already and I think it's time you were moving on out of this town."

"Sheriff," the stranger said in that same mocking tone of voice, "I can't be moving on. I'm a resident here now. I'm in business here. I just bought this here hotel. In fact, since I live here and do business here, it's your job to protect me."

Bridges drew his gun and cocked it and made certain the stranger saw what he was doing.

"Stranger," he said, his eyes glaring, "we don't even know your name, and we don't want to know it."

"My name," the stranger said, "is Siempre."

Bridges raised his gun real slow. "Get up and get out," he said.

Still sitting in his chair, the stranger turned slowly to face him.

"Never," he said. "You'll have to kill me first."

Bridges glanced around the room. "You heard him, boys," he said, and then he took careful aim and fired.

The blast of the Colt sent echoes booming all around that room. The stranger jumped, spinning a little to the side. Sheriff Bridges was the best shot in that town. Folks there used to joke that he could shoot the label off a bottle and never crack the glass. This time he'd fired at the stranger's right arm, and he'd hit him too. Plenty of folks saw the bullet strike his arm and pass right on through it, and then bury itself in the plaster of the wall behind him.

But the sheriff hadn't figured on the stranger—Siempre, as he called himself—being left-handed. And he hadn't counted at all on what happened next.

That stranger's gun appeared in his left hand like it had jumped there all by itself. It seemed to have a life of its own. One second it was there in the stranger's holster, the next second it was blazing away, five shots, coming so close together that they sounded like one long explosion.

And when the sound died away, Sheriff Emmett Bridges was lying on the floor in a pool of his own blood, and so was Will Ash and Sam Frederickson and Andy Benjamin. And so was Tom Pinkwater too.

The stranger's gun had picked them out in the crowd, just like the hand of fate, and each one had a neat bullet hole in him, pumping blood. Nobody else had been touched.

The law in Two Trails was dead, and the realization of that left everybody there in the Elite frozen with shock. They just stared at the bodies and nobody moved.

Over near the table where the stranger was sitting, young Billy Wagner looked from him to Clayton Bannister who hadn't moved from his place near the door. Something inside the boy—maybe the suddenness or the violence of what had happened—made him want to stand beside that big man, and he quietly slipped around behind other folks and made his way toward the door.

The stranger dropped his gun back in its holster. He didn't even bother to reload it, the way any other gunfighter would have done, as if he had such contempt for the people of that town that he knew nobody would speak a word or lift a hand against him. And maybe he was right. They just looked from him to the bodies and then back to him again.

"There a banker here?" the stranger said.

T. J. Mulvaney stepped forward, the sweat shining on his face.

The man in black waved a careless hand toward the floor and the table. "Best pick up that man's gold," he said, "and put it in the bank for his relatives. And remember that you're a witness I paid up fair and square for this hotel."

Mulvaney scrabbled the coins together into the pockets of his coat just as quick as he could.

The stranger looked around at the bodies on the floor.

"Too bad your lawmen fired first and wounded an innocent man who had to shoot back in self-defense."

That reminded folks of two things. First was that Tom Pinkwater had been shot in cold blood, and that only after the stranger had humiliated him. Second was the wound in the stranger's right arm. There was blood there, all right, on the sleeve just above the elbow, but there was no sign of an injury as the stranger leaned that arm comfortably on the table.

"Barkeep," he called over to Terry Phelan, who helped out with meals at the Elite, "bring me a fresh plate of food. This one's cold. And then move these bodies out of here. I like my place kept clean. And the rest of you," he added in a louder voice, "you just carry on with your business. First round of drinks is on the house. Just step right over to the bar and get yourselves fixed up."

Folks just shuffled from one foot to the other, not knowing which way to move. Then one man poked another and jerked his head toward the bar, and there was some general movement in that direction.

"Just one other thing," the stranger said, and everyone turned back to face him.

"You heard my name once," he said. "I don't want you to forget it." His eyes moved around the room, taking in the whole scene. "My name is Siempre, and I'm here to stay."

That's how the man named Siempre came to the town of Two Trails. He just came riding in from nowhere, looking like a ghost— "a ha'nt," Old Jed Tree had called him when he first laid eyes on him —and then his guns were blazing, every law officer in the town was dead, fear rode high in every heart, and Siempre was the king.

For a few days after his arrival, nothing much happened. Pete Schumann, who filled the roles of barber and undertaker both, worked on the bodies all through Saturday night, making them decent, and all day Sunday you could hear the hammering as the coffins were hastily constructed, and there was a multiple funeral on Monday morning. That disrupted the town's regular routine somewhat, but by that afternoon things were pretty much back to normal. There was some angry talk, to be sure, but it was all done in private. A few people even drifted into the Elite and were relieved to see that Terry Phelan was still behind the bar, but he knew nothing more about the stranger than anyone else did.

What did the people of Two Trails actually know about this stranger who called himself Siempre?

All over that town, people compared notes and discovered that they knew very little indeed.

They knew his name, or what he claimed was his name. Siempre.

The Spanish word meaning Forever. But was he Spanish? Some said he might be. Look at his clothes, they said, dark but kind of showy. Some thought there was a foreign-looking cast to his skin but nobody felt too sure about that. Others swore they'd heard some kind of accent in his voice—maybe Spanish, maybe something else—but it was hard to say just what it was. When they thought about it, most folks thought they'd heard that accent after all, but nobody could say for sure what it was. The one thing everybody agreed on was that Siempre, whoever he was, had traveled a long distance getting to Two Trails.

What else did they know?

He was a big man, bigger than almost any man they'd ever laid eyes on. He had a jagged scar, like a streak of lightning, down the left side of his face. He had black hair and a black moustache and eyes as black as coal. He was the fastest gun anybody there had ever seen or even heard tell of. He didn't mind killing in cold blood, and they knew he'd be willing to kill again the same way if anybody crossed him. And, murderer or not, he had no intentions of leaving the town.

They knew he was living in a room on the first floor of the hotel—Terry Phelan had whispered that to them—and having his meals sent up. And he had his revolver and his rifle with him. Terry had seen them in the room.

Beyond that much, for the first couple of days, they knew nothing.

So they waited, nervously, to see when he'd appear again and to find out what he'd want next. That, at least, was the one thing everybody was sure of: that stranger would want something else.

It didn't take long to find out what it was.

4

Clayton Bannister, acting the role of a silent and mild-mannered newcomer known as John Nelson, had faded out of the Elite as soon as Siempre made his little speech reminding everybody of his name.

It wasn't the sound of gunfire that drove him away—he'd heard plenty of that. And it wasn't the sight of five dead bodies, bodies that a minute before had been living, breathing men, or the sight of their life's blood leaking out, or even the wantonness and viciousness of the killing. It was none of those things. But it was something real enough, just as real as bullets and blood, and it made him leave that place to go and face it by himself.

He was out on the wooden sidewalk, making his way back toward the east end of town, when he heard a light step on the planks behind him. He turned and looked down into the face of Billy Wagner.

"Where you going, John?" the boy said. From their first meeting, it had seemed natural to both of them for the youngster to call the older man by his first name.

Clayton Bannister looked like a terrible sadness was weighing down his shoulders. He looked into the boy's face and his wide eyes for a long minute before answering.

"I have business to tend to, son," he said quietly.

"But, John," the boy said at once, with something strange in his voice that even he had never heard before, "ain't you gonna do something about them killings? That stranger, he just gunned down the sheriff and the deputies and Tom Pinkwater too, just gunned 'em down in cold blood. You seen it yourself."

Clayton Bannister studied the boy's face, and he saw in it the shock and the pain of sudden manhood, and outrage at random violence, and frustration at his own powerlessness, and puzzlement at his own lack of understanding how such things could happen in his hitherto safe world.

"I saw it," the big man said. "I saw every bit of it. What I didn't see was anyone else moving his hand to draw a gun. All I saw was the people of Two Trails stepping up to the bar to drink that man's liquor, and stepping over the bodies of their friends to do it. I didn't stay to drink his liquor, son."

"I know that, John. But—"

He stopped himself when he heard a step behind him and saw the man's gaze look beyond his head. He turned to look too and saw Old Jed Tree coming along the sidewalk. Jed looked pretty feeble and he kept one gnarled hand sort of gliding along the wall, but he was coming strong and steady. The man and boy waited till the old fellow came up to them.

"I seen you stepping out," Old Jed said to Billy. "I come along to see where a boy could be going to in such a hurry."

He was talking to the boy but a look passed between the two men to say that they both understood.

"You was coming after me," young Billy said, "but I was going after John here."

"What for, son?" the old man said.

"Why, to fetch him back and get him to put things to rights here in town."

The boy looked from one to the other while both men looked at him.

Clayton Bannister put a hand on the boy's shoulder. It was a big hand but he touched the boy gently.

"Son, maybe I was going off to fetch somebody back myself," he said.

Now the boy studied his face before speaking again. It was silent there in the street, nothing moving, only the sun beating down on the road.

"But there ain't no one but yourself to fetch back," the boy said at last.

Clayton Bannister looked away then and all three of them dropped their gaze to the wooden sidewalk.

Then Old Jed Tree told the youngster to run on home to the family he was living with and leave his elders to do some talking.

The boy hesitated, then started slowly away. But before he was gone across the road, he left Clayton Bannister with one more comment.

"It's gun talk that's wanted," he said. Then, hands shoved deep in his pockets and head bowed beneath the heat of the sun, he walked off toward the other side of the street.

"The youngster's right, o' course," Old Jed said.

"I know it," Clayton Bannister said. He had turned away and was looking down the length of the empty sidewalk.

"And you're the fella."

"Why's that?"

"Why, look at yourself. Look at the size and the cut of you. Look at the way you wear your belt low for an easy draw. Look at the strings in the back o' your hand, just ready to twitch up a gun. I know the signs. You've done some shooting."

"And if I have?"

"There's more to do."

"Supposing I have," the big man said. He was still looking down that empty street. "What if I'm finished with it?"

"But it ain't finished," the old-timer said, and there might have been some sadness in his voice too, enough to match Clayton Bannister's own.

"I can say it is."

"You can *say* it."

Clayton Bannister turned around to face the old man.

"It's not my fight. I don't live here. I'll be moving on from this town."

"Question is, which way will you be going when you leave? There's only the two trails out of here."

"I don't like killing. I've seen it, plenty of it, and I don't like it. Maybe I don't want to see any more of it."

"Man like you never does. But sometimes it just stands there in your path and won't step aside."

"Like you, old-timer?" Clayton Bannister said, and there was a distant hint of a smile on his lips, a signal that their talk was ended.

"I ain't blocking your path, son," Old Jed said calmly. "You was going the other direction. I'm just seeing you on your way."

He was living in a room built onto the back of Jack Weaver's big old farmhouse. It had its own door and so he could come and go at will without answering to anybody. He kept to himself, and the few people who asked Jack Weaver who this John Nelson was got little information because Weaver himself knew nothing. Nelson took some of his meals with them, if he happened to be in the house at mealtime, and paid for what he ate at the end of the week. The man paid his rent regular and didn't cause no trouble, that's all the farmer knew, and he and his wife were glad of the extra bit coming in.

He spent some time in town, mostly just watching, talking hardly at all. He ate some meals at the Elite. He bought a shirt once from Felix Hart's Double T Emporium, and some ammunition a couple of times—for practice, he'd murmured to Felix, as if a man needed an excuse to buy bullets—and he took a couple of drinks at each of the saloons in town, and he brought in a bridle to be mended one time at Feeley's. That's about what people knew of John Nelson in Two Trails. He kept everything else to himself.

He spent some days riding into the desert and some other days exploring the foothills. He always rode alone. He always took his guns with him and his bedroll too, and some nights he didn't return to Weaver's farmhouse. Every now and again somebody from the town might spot a lone rider in the distance who had the size and the shape of John Nelson. The rider would stop his horse and raise one arm high in salute, the way folks do who live in the open spaces where another human being is a sight to take note of, but then he'd lower that arm and tug the reins and ride off the other way.

The sky and the open land were his friends, the companions to his thoughts. They asked no questions of him, demanded nothing except his mute respect, which they had, and they let him be. Sometimes he shot a jackrabbit or a grouse and made his meal in the open. Sometimes he rolled up beside a guttered fire at night and wondered at the stars.

He wondered about other things too. Sometimes he wondered who he'd been as a youngster. Maybe he'd been like Billy Wagner, wise beyond his years and hungry for greater wisdom still. He wondered who he'd be if he lived to grow old. Jed Tree? Maybe.

He wondered about the things he felt he had to do, and about the things he felt he needn't.

And he wondered when he'd die. And where. And how. And what a world could be like that did not contain him.

Some of those nights in the open, he didn't sleep at all. He lay there looking at the stars, and the stars, cold and silent and far, far away, looked back and refused to yield their answers.

It was the Thursday after the funeral, just after breakfast time, and Clayton Bannister was heading out for the open spaces when he saw young Billy Wagner sitting a horse up ahead, waiting for him.

"Where ya riding, John?"

The man drew rein beside the boy's horse.

"Just going off to be by myself. Noplace in particular."

"Can I come?"

Clayton Bannister cast a critical eye over the boy and the horse he was riding.

"Where'd you get that nag?"

"Belongs to Feeley. He said I could take him and give him some exercise."

"Long as you don't kill him, right?"

"Well, yeah." The boy tried to hold back his grin but it showed a little at the corners of his mouth. "He'll be all right. Long as I don't run him too hard."

"What's that rolled up behind you?"

"Slicker and bedroll." The boy said it in a matter-of-fact voice. "Got a side of bacon too, and the makings for pan bread."

The man said nothing.

"Got coffee too," the boy added, but now he sounded less sure of himself, the boy in him peeking out from behind the man he would someday be.

"You're ready for a trip," Clayton Bannister said.

Now it was the boy's turn to say nothing and only return the man's look.

"You ever sleep in the open?"

"Plenty of times."

"You're lying."

"Well, a few."

"You're sure that horse isn't going to die anytime soon?"

"I'm sure."

The man could have kept the exchange going longer, and part of him wanted to, wanted to wear down the boy's resolve, but another part of him realized that he'd already given in.

"Well, I guess you can come, then," he said.

Without another word he clucked to his horse and continued in the direction he'd been going, and the boy fell in behind him.

They traveled like that for two hours, sometimes walking the horses and sometimes letting them canter. Neither one spoke at all and Clayton Bannister never once looked behind him to see how the boy was doing. The sound of the other horse's steps was there, a constant presence at his back, and that was enough.

The sun was hot, growing hotter as the day wore on toward noon. They were heading westward, with the sun at their backs, and the ground began to rise gradually before them. Ahead lay the mountains, bare and rocky in patches, dark and green with spiky firs in other places.

If the boy hadn't been there, and that sorry horse he was riding, the man would have made better time, let his own horse find a comfortable pace that would cover miles without wearing out either one of them. That way he would have reached the pines before the sun reached the top of the sky.

But he found now that he didn't mind this slower pace. It was comfortable. It was good, in a way, hearing that other horse coming along steadily behind him, good hearing it in those otherwise empty places. Good too that the boy knew enough not to chatter, not to talk at all, in fact. That struck the man especially, that the boy knew silence was the right thing for this time. He asked no questions, made no demands, just came right along at the same pace, maybe thinking the same thoughts.

The man wondered a little at that. Could it be the boy was enough like him to be thinking the same things? Here they were, riding along easy, in an easy silence, looking at the same ground and the same mountains ahead. Maybe all men had the same thoughts, looking at the same places the way the two of them were doing right now.

And then something occurred to Clayton Bannister.

He reined in his horse and, without turning around, waited for the boy to come up. After a moment, the boy's horse came alongside, but the boy didn't look at Bannister and the old horse just kept going.

After a minute, the man fell in behind him. And after a while, the boy spoke a word to his horse and urged him into a canter, and behind them the man did the same.

Now the boy would have the same sight of the land, the same feel of it, his view unobstructed by another human being, and only the good sound of another rider coming along behind.

They rode like that for another hour or so, still not speaking a word.

It was the boy who changed direction and headed a little more to the north. The man, riding easy in the saddle, with the comfortable creak of leather beneath him, let his own horse follow. And after another half hour they came to a line of firs that offered welcome shade from that fierce sun, and a tiny creek of clear water that made a cool and pretty sound in that vast and empty silence.

The boy swung from the saddle and led his horse forward to drink before he drank himself.

The man watched this, then swung down to the ground. He leaned his right arm on his own saddle for a minute and looked at the boy crouching beside the horse. Then he led his own eager horse forward and let him drink beside the other.

After a bit, the horses finished drinking, snorted, and backed off to pull at the tough mountain grass.

Before he bent forward to drink himself, the boy said, still without turning around, "I'll fix some grub, if you like."

Clayton Bannister knelt down beside him.

"I'll make the coffee," he said.

Together, the two of them leaned forward to taste the icy water.

"Where do you come from?" the boy asked him at last.

It was dark now and they were higher up the slopes, the fire crackling yellow against the dark and their blankets pulled tight around their shoulders. They were drinking coffee.

"My business," the man said.

"Where you heading, then?"

"Don't know yet."

"When will you know?"

"Soon, I guess."

The boy made a wordless grunt, which was the right response.

In the silence, one of the horses sneezed.

"You're gonna have to kill Siempre, you know."

The man said nothing to that.

"Well, you are."

The man poured himself another cup of the thick, strong coffee, then filled up the boy's cup too.

"Tell me about it," he said, and took a drink from the cup. He wrapped his hands around it to keep them warm.

The boy pulled his blanket a little tighter and edged a little closer to the fire, and then he started in to talk.

Clayton Bannister listened without saying a word, and anybody watching him would have figured he was seriously intent on nothing but that cup of coffee he was drinking.

The man who called himself Forever, the boy told him, had finally appeared again in Two Trails on Monday evening. He'd eaten his supper downstairs in the Elite where anybody who cared to come by and have a look could see him. And he looked like a man who didn't have a care in the world. He ate hearty and he drank near half a bottle of whiskey and he did it all at a table near the front windows, the ones facing on the sidewalk, and he even had Terry Phelan bring a candle for the table so's he'd show up plain as day. It was like he was showing himself to the town, almost like he was daring every-body to come and have a look at the man who'd committed murder in cold blood and didn't give a hang about it. He was making a point and making it plain: those murders and that big funeral that morning didn't mean as much to him as the death of a flea-bitten prairie rat.

And everybody in that town got the point, all right. They all stepped real quiet when they passed that window and a good many of them actually went right on inside and bellied up to the bar the way they always had and bought themselves a drink.

And nobody said a word about the killings. There they were, drinking in the same room with the killer, and T. J. Mulvaney, the banker, drinking there with them, and nobody spoke a word. And they all knew it, and they were all busy keeping their eyes down while they made polite conversation, but they all knew it.

The man who called himself Siempre sat there at that table with his whiskey till the last man had strolled out of the place that night. A couple of them sort of nodded in his direction as they left. He looked right at each one of them in return, but it was more like he was looking right through them.

And then the next morning, Tuesday, he went to work.

Folks saw him coming out of the Elite around nine o'clock. He came down those steps easy as running water, wearing those same black clothes he'd arrived in, and angled across the street. Everybody could see he had those bulging black saddlebags thrown across his right shoulder. He walked like a man who'd known the town all his life, and he was heading straight for Felix Hart's Double T Emporium, the biggest store in town.

He arrived there at the very second Felix Hart was throwing his doors open for the start of the day's business. Felix Hart took one long look at that scarred face and those dark eyes and those saddlebags and the butt of that black gun. Then he backed off like a man who'd just had a close-up look at a ghost, and that stranger followed him inside.

He wasn't there but five minutes, and when he came out on the street again, the man called Siempre owned the Double T Emporium, lock, stock, and barrel, and he'd paid for it with more of those shining gold coins from his saddlebags.

He came out in the street again and crossed over—a couple of folks had to pull up their buckboards mighty sharp to avoid running into him—and walked right straight on to Feeley's harness and blacksmith shop. And when he got there, he went inside for about five minutes, and when he came out, he was the owner of that place too.

He did that seven times more, just going up and down the street. Some places he was inside only five minutes, and other places took him as much as maybe twenty, but every time he came out, he owned that business. Everybody was afraid of that gun and the look in his eye and they sold out without complaining.

Then he went back to the Elite and sat in the window and ate a hearty midday meal.

When he'd eaten, he went back to see Martin Feeley, who worked for him now, and waited while Feeley saddled up that black horse. The stranger's rifle had been hanging there with the saddle all this while, and Feeley told folks later that Siempre never even checked it. He just knew it was still loaded and clean. Then he rode off without a word, and folks that saw him going said he was headed in the direction of Fred Mitchum's horse ranch.

He came back about suppertime, and nobody in Two Trails doubted that he'd bought out Fred Mitchum too, and that would have taken one heck of a lot of gold.

That was Tuesday.

On Wednesday, Siempre visited most of the other shops and businesses in town. By noon, he owned everything worth owning, and almost everybody in that town was working for him.

And in the afternoon, he went to see T. J. Mulvaney in the bank. He was in there close to two hours, but when he came outside again, he owned the bank too. And that was the bank, of course, where all the former businessmen of Two Trails had quickly deposited the very same gold he'd paid them earlier. The same bank, too, that held liens for money loaned out on nearly every building, big or little, in Two Trails.

Any time he wanted, just any time at all, Siempre could snap his fingers and close down that town.

There was a little coffee left in the pot. Clayton Bannister divided it equally between his cup and the boy's.

The boy swallowed some of the hot coffee and then looked at the man's dark face in the flickering light of the fire.

"You gotta kill him, John," he said.

Clayton Bannister looked deeply into the yellow flames of the fire, as if that primitive element might hold the answers to the questions that troubled him. He leaned forward and fed a few more branches into the fire and waited till the flames had grown a little brighter. Then at last he spoke, but he still did not look at the boy.

"Tell me what people are saying."

"Don't need to think too hard on that," the boy answered solemnly. "Everybody's afraid, 'specially now with Emmett Bridges and all the deputies dead. It's not just that Siempre killed 'em, it's the being without law that's got folks down. So when Siempre went to visit, they all just handed over what he wanted."

"Any talk of killing?"

"Some."

"Any plans?"

"Nope."

They were silent for a while again, watching the flames together.

"Any talk of me?"

"Sure."

The man looked up and the boy's eyes met his. Each saw the same flame from the fire dancing in the eyes of the other.

"Old Jed Tree," the boy said.

Clayton Bannister nodded.

The boy shifted on the ground, seeking a more comfortable position.

"There's one other thing," he said. "Jed told me to be sure and tell you this. There was a meeting of some of the people last night at T. J. Mulvaney's house. Mulvaney didn't call the meeting, but folks just sort of went on out there anyway to talk things over and see what their friends are gonna do. And Mulvaney told 'em something that Siempre said. He said he'd own the whole town, every building and every square inch of land. But that wasn't the main thing he was after in Two Trails."

Clayton Bannister was watching the boy closely now and there was a look in his fire-bright eyes that said he knew what was coming.

"Siempre said there was nothing he wanted in Two Trails as much as he wanted Mary Cantrell."

The man closed his eyes for a second. When he opened them, they seemed to have borrowed some of the simple, primitive light from the fire.

"Better get some sleep," he told the boy quietly.

He lay down on the ground and hunched the blanket close around his shoulders. After a minute, the boy did the same.

"Long day tomorrow," the man said. "We'll start at dawn."

"Sure," the boy said. "You know where Mary Cantrell's farm is?"

"I know."

Clayton Bannister lay awake a long time that night. He studied the stars all that while, but the stars didn't tell him a thing.

5

Nobody in Two Trails at that time knew exactly how long Mary Cantrell had lived there, but it must have been maybe eight or ten years. To most folks, she'd just always seemed to be a part of the place. Nobody knew her all that well, either, but she was pretty near the most popular person in that town, man or woman.

She came into town once a week, maybe, to sell her farm produce and buy supplies, and she came in to attend church on Sundays, and if the church was having a Sunday dinner or something of the sort, she'd be there then too. But other than those times, folks never saw much of her. Even so, everybody knew her and liked her. She always had a smile and a friendly word and a question about the rest of the family, that sort of neighborly thing. Even the young fellows who worked on her farm, helping out with the heavy chores, didn't know much about her.

Maybe there was just nothing to know.

But everybody admired her and liked her. As for admiring her, nobody could help feeling admiration for a woman who could get by on her own in the West, the West not being too friendly a place for anybody in those times, let alone a woman. And a youngish woman at that. There was endless speculation about her age but no one knew for sure what it was.

As for liking her, there was nothing not to like. She was just as pretty as anything, too, with a smile like a sunrise on Sunday morning. And she had the nicest eyes, dark, but warm and soothing, somehow. When she looked at you with those eyes, you felt she was looking into your heart and she understood all the things about you you could never bring yourself to say. There was never any nonsense in her, either, and she dressed kind of plain, no fripperies or anything. She never needed stuff like that. She had those eyes.

She had her place fixed up real nice and civilized, too, just like her, with flowers and grass and a white fence in the front. She was waiting by the fence when Clayton Bannister and the boy rode up the next morning.

"Good morning," she called out before they'd even dismounted. She favored them both with a smile but it was no secret that it put a strain on her to produce it.

"Morning, Miz Cantrell."

He lifted the front of his hat and came to stand in front of her.

"I heard about your difficulty, ma'am, and I came to tell you I'll do my best to set things to rights in Two Trails before you're bothered anymore."

"I haven't been bothered yet," Mary Cantrell said, her voice showing the same strain as her smile, "but I'm expecting that man to ride in here anytime now. The boys who work for me have told me everything he's been doing. And they told me what he said to Mr. Mulvaney."

"Yes, ma'am," Clayton Bannister said.

"It's like he's saving me up for last, and the waiting for it is getting to me."

"Yes, ma'am, that's why I came by to tell you I'll do what I can."

He lifted his hand toward his hat and started to say goodbye.

"Wait," Mary Cantrell said. "What are you going to do?"

"I'll do what I have to do," Clayton Bannister said, and a hard edge crept into his voice as he said it.

"He's gonna kill him," Billy Wagner said.

Mary Cantrell dropped her gaze to the ground at that. When she looked up, she said softly, "It'll take a lot to kill Forever."

"I'll do my best," Clayton Bannister said.

"I have an idea—"

"I'll do my best," he said again.

Then he did lift his hat in farewell and remounted his horse. In a minute, he and the boy were galloping off in the direction of Two Trails.

Young Billy Wagner was a brave boy and didn't hesitate a second to carry out the man's instructions.

Long before Clayton Bannister appeared in town himself, the boy came galloping down the street, pushing that wheezing horse to the limit and attracting as much attention as possible. He went the length of the street, then turned around and hightailed it back the other way, whipping his hat across the horse's flanks all the while. He finally came to a halt in front of the rooming house where Old Jed Tree lived.

Within fifteen minutes, every man, woman, and child in that town knew that John Nelson was heading this way and that he was gunning for the man who called himself Forever.

And if everybody else knew it, that meant that Siempre knew it too.

"Siempre!"

Clayton Bannister's shout seemed to fill that dusty street, cutting through the sunbaked air like the cold steel blade of a knife.

He stood out there by himself in the middle of the road, a dark figure in the blinding sunlight. He had his feet spread apart, planted solidly on the ground. His hat was pulled low to shade his eyes. His right hand hung loose and easy, near his gun.

The street itself was otherwise empty, but there were faces looking out from every doorway and every window on both sides.

All eyes were fixed on the front doors of the Elite.

Siempre did not appear.

The town waited for Bannister to call again.

But Bannister just stood there.

Hidden in the doorways and shops, some folks began whispering to each other. "Maybe Siempre didn't hear him," they said. "That Nelson fellow better call him out again, and good luck to him!" they said.

But Bannister only waited.

The sun beat down like a hammer on the road, making it shimmer a little even to someone looking across only the width of it. The heat made wet clothing cling to skin, and every man had to raise a nervous hand to wipe the shine from his face.

Bannister, alone out there in the road, didn't move.

And then, at long last, the batwing doors of the Elite swung wide and Siempre stepped onto the sidewalk. He crossed slowly to the steps and turned to look at Clayton Bannister.

For a long time, neither one of them said a word.

"It's time," Bannister called at last. "It's time, Siempre."

"Is it?" the man in black answered, in that familiar voice that seemed so hushed and yet carried so far.

"I've seen enough now," Bannister said, "and I've waited long enough. Plenty long. You can't have this town, Siempre, you can't make it yours. Come out in the road and we'll settle this."

"I already have this town," Siempre answered. "I own this town and every soul in it."

"No," said the man the townsfolk knew as John Nelson. "There are still a few you don't have. A few you'll never have."

Siempre laughed. It was a loud and ugly sound, like the bark of a vicious dog, and as dark as night in that sunny street.

"Come on, Siempre, see if you're faster than I am. See if you can win the thing you really want."

Siempre reacted to that. He stepped down to the road.

"I'll kill you," he said.

"No," Clayton Bannister told him. "You won't."

His words barely had time to travel across the open space that separated them before Siempre's gun was in his hand and spitting fire. No man there—and every one of them was watching mighty close—could even see that hand move or that black gun leave the holster. It just flew up and exploded, all in the same second. The blast of it roared through the silent town, the sound filling that empty street.

In the same instant, Bannister dropped, slanched, and spun to the side, his own gun blazing once.

The two shots came so close together, they might have been a single shot from the same gun.

And the two men were still alive.

Siempre was crouched, ready to spring, his gun held out in front of him.

Clayton Bannister's position was identical.

Since it was Siempre's left arm that was stretched out, his left hand holding the gun, matching Clayton Bannister's right arm and hand, the two men might have been mirror images of each other.

Why didn't they fire again?

Everybody watching realized then what was holding the two fighters back. It must be that neither one of them had ever missed his target before with his first shot, and now the two of them were so surprised, they had to stop and think that over for a bit before doing anything else.

Then Siempre straightened up. He just uncoiled like a snake and stood up to his full height, completely exposed. He still had his left hand out in front of him, still had that ugly black gun pointing at Clayton Bannister, but he looked like a man completely confident of victory, immune to any sort of danger.

And then Clayton Bannister straightened up too, the exact same way Siempre had.

They eyed each other.

"You see, gunfighter?" Siempre called out at last. The scorn was loud in his voice. "You see you can't kill me?"

"You see me standing here?" Clayton Bannister answered back.

Siempre raised his chin a little at that, as if the meaning of the other man's answer had struck him hard.

"All right, gunfighter," Siempre said. "I'm going to flip this gun in the air, and when it comes back to my hand, I'm going to fire a couple of bullets into your heart."

"You will," Bannister said, "you will, if that gun ever gets back to your hand."

Siempre laughed again, then everyone saw that gun of his just swinging loose on his trigger finger hooked through the guard. He let it hang for a few seconds, then suddenly the gun was twirling straight up from his hand, turning over and over, going high above his head.

Clayton Bannister did nothing, and those few silent seconds stretched out to seem as long as anyone there watching it had lived in all his years. That gun just seemed to keep turning and Bannister only watched it, not moving at all himself. He was an honorable man, everyone thought, that must be it, and for those few seconds, Siempre was unarmed and so Bannister couldn't shoot him then.

Everybody watched the gun, and knew all the while that it was another sign of Siempre's contempt for every one of them, showing his confidence, his control of the situation.

The gun spun upwards and then at long last it reached the peak of its arc and started back down toward Siempre's waiting hand. Every eye was on it. When that gun struck his hand again, it was going to belch fire and destruction and very likely mean the instant death of his opponent.

Over and over that gun turned, taking an eternity to come back down.

Then Siempre's hand moved lightning-fast and snatched it right out of the air, and it looked like that gun was already blazing fire.

Four times it roared, the blasts coming closer together than any man there had ever heard before.

But in that same instant, Clayton Bannister was moving, and his gun was blazing with the same eager ferocity as Siempre's weapon. He hurled himself forward on the ground, almost diving straight into the line of fire, and his finger squeezed off four shots that matched the other man's one for one.

But Siempre, with that same animal-like grace that made his movements almost invisible, was spinning and twisting away from the line of Bannister's fire. Four shots from Bannister's gun whizzed past him.

And when the roaring had stopped, both men were still alive. They were still crouching, guns still extended toward each other, just like before. It seemed impossible that they should both be still breathing after a volley of shots like that, but they were.

Now each of them had one shot left.

Siempre straightened up again, same as he'd done before, but this time he let his left arm drop to his side. He was still holding the gun, of course, but this time it was pointing at the ground.

"So, gunfighter," he said. He said it more quietly than he'd ever spoken before, and for that reason it sounded all the more threatening and frightening. "So, gunfighter. You think you can kill me. But you are wrong. You can never kill me."

"I'll kill you, Siempre," Clayton Bannister said, and his voice perfectly matched that of the other man in its sound of dark intention.

"No," Siempre said. "Because you are already dead."

He never raised his hand, never lifted his gun from where it hung beside his leg. All he did was twist his wrist and the barrel of the gun jumped upward and roared out once more.

In the same breath, Clayton Bannister fired his final shot.

Neither one of them moved this time, as they had before.

And neither one of them moved as the sound of the double explosion faded away.

The folks watching from windows and doorways waited for one or the other of them to topple over dead. One of them had to have killed the other, or maybe both bullets had found their mark, the two men were so equally matched.

But they just went right on standing there. You could see both of them breathing hard and staring hard at each other, like they didn't believe what was happening. But there they were, both of them just as real and alive as they'd been before, and no mistake about it.

Six shots from each of them, at short range in an empty street in broad daylight, and the two of them still standing up. Every man there said to himself, this is something to tell my grandchildren about someday. I'm witnessing a great moment in history, and that's a fact.

Finally, Siempre dropped his empty gun back in its holster. A moment later, Clayton Bannister did the same.

"So, gunfighter," the man in black said. His words were just the same as before, but a man with imagination might almost have thought there was a hint of respect in his voice this time. "So. At last I have a worthy opponent."

"We're not done with this, Siempre," Clayton Bannister called across the space that separated them. "We'll meet again and settle this once and for all."

Siempre barked out a laugh.

"You're not afraid to die?" he asked.

"I'll die one day," the other man answered. "But it won't be at your hands."

"We'll see, gunfighter. We'll see."

They eyed each other closely.

"When would you like to meet again, gunfighter? Tell me when. You name the time and I'll name the place." He was smiling now, the smile growing broader by the second, beaming confidence in himself and outright scorn for everyone else, especially for someone with the nerve to challenge his superiority. "You just tell me when, gunfighter."

"Dawn," Clayton Bannister answered. "Meet me at dawn." He was not smiling.

"As you wish, gunfighter," Siempre said. "And I choose the graveyard as the place."

"That'll suit me just fine," Bannister said. "The graveyard at dawn."

"You'll die then, of course," Siempre said. "That's the one thing you can count on. But I want you to remember something from now until then. Something for you to think about besides your own death."

Clayton Bannister never took his eyes from Siempre but he made no reply to that.

There was a long silence. Everybody watching and listening held their breath.

"I know you," Siempre said.

Folks with a good view of Siempre's face thought his smile returned and grew even wider as he said it.

"I know you, Clayton Bannister."

The silence after that was like the stillness of the desert with not even the wind moving across its face.

And then Clayton Bannister just turned and walked away. He just turned on his heel and pointed his back at the man in black, showing contempt in his own silent way, and walked off down that empty street toward the alley where he'd tethered his horse out of the line of fire.

He disappeared from view for a few seconds when he went into the alley, and then he was back there in the street, mounted on his horse and heading out of town, his back straight and proud as he rode.

Behind him, the man who called himself Siempre let out a roar of mocking laughter.

6

The night was cool and clear and the sky was filled with stars. A crescent moon hung like a knife blade in the sky.

Mary Cantrell stood on the top step of her porch. Her eyes searched the stars in the sky, they searched the road that passed in front of the house, they combed the hills that formed her horizon. She had been standing there for pretty near an hour. Once, as the air grew chill and sharp with the disappearance of the sun, she'd gone back inside and fetched out a sheepskin coat to put around her shoulders. But then she'd returned to the porch to keep on watching.

The evenings didn't usually grow so cold there in the hills at that time of year, and the air felt all the colder for following the burning heat of the day. Funny thing, how a body feels something all the more sharply after living with its opposite for even a short while.

She lifted up her head and looked to the right when she heard the sound of horses in the road. After a while, she could make out the shapes of two horses and riders moving toward her from the direction of town. Her heart started beating a little faster at that, but in a minute or two she was able to recognize them.

It was young Billy Wagner and Old Jed Tree, and out of respect for Old Jed's ancient bones, they'd come all the way from Two Trails at a walking pace.

"Evening, Miz Cantrell," Billy said as he slid to the ground in front of her steps. Beyond him, Old Jed was easing himself more slowly to the ground.

"Evening, Billy. Evening, Mr. Tree."

"Will it be all right if I let the horses in here?" Billy asked, pointing at the nearby gate.

"Sure will," Mary Cantrell said. "And it's nice to have visitors all the way out here. You've had a long ride, and no supper to make you strong for it, I'll warrant. You just get those horses settled, Billy, and I'll fix up something hot for you to eat. Here, Mr. Tree, let me give you a hand up these steps. They're a little unsteady."

The steps were no more unsteady than Old Jed Tree himself, and both of them knew it, but he graciously accepted her helping hand.

A few minutes later, the three of them were settled at the table near the fire and a pot of rabbit stew was bubbling and filling the house with its warm smell. Mary Cantrell poured out coffee for the three of them. They all took a mouthful and the boy and the old man nodded their thanks before anyone spoke further.

Then Mary Cantrell set her cup down on the table.

"Is there any news?" she said, and they all three knew she'd been longing to ask that question all the while she was being hospitable.

"Yes, ma'am," Billy said. He kept his hands around the cup to warm them, and started in to recount what had happened that afternoon in town, telling it straight without a lot of fuss or embellishment.

When he got to the end of it, Mary Cantrell said nothing at first. All she did was get up and fetch the pot of coffee and refill Billy's cup and the old man's. She hadn't touched her own since tasting it the first time.

They were all lost in thought for a minute or two. Then Mary Cantrell asked, "What was that about Siempre calling John Nelson by another name?"

"Clayton Bannister," Old Jed Tree said. It was the first time he'd spoken since coming to the house. "That's his name, his real name. Clayton Bannister."

"How do you know that?" the young woman asked.

Old Jed either grimaced or smiled, it was hard to tell which.

"I've lived a long time," he said slowly, "and I've seen a lot of things. You pick up plenty of information when you live a long time, and that's a fact."

"Why would he come to Two Trails and give folks another name?"

"Private reasons, I reckon," the boy said. He sounded older than his years—old enough, anyway, to know that a man could have pretty good private reasons for doing what other folks might consider strange.

Old Jed nodded in agreement.

"But what about that other man, Siempre? How did he know John Nelson's real name?"

Old Jed took a long drink of hot coffee before he answered, as if he might be fixing up a proper reply before speaking.

"Could be he's lived even longer than me," he said at last. Then he looked deliberately at the pot on the fire. "Smells mighty good there. Think it's ready yet?"

Mary Cantrell rose from the table and served up food for the three of them. The man and boy both put away heaping plates of stew but she barely touched her own.

They ate in silence, but it was a friendly silence, as warm as the smell of good food and the heat of a fire. They all three knew that the menfolk were there to keep the woman from spending a night alone in that house with a threat hanging over her head.

When they'd finished eating and she had poured out the first cups from a fresh pot of coffee, Mary Cantrell said, "Where do you suppose Clayton Bannister is now?"

"Riding the hills, I reckon," young Billy said.

"He's riding the hills, all right," Old Jed said, "but he'll be coming along here when he's done with that."

"He'll come here? Do you really think so?" Mary Cantrell said. She made no effort to hide her sudden pleasure and relief.

"I reckon," the old man said.

It was about ten minutes after that when they heard the sound of galloping hoofbeats outside in the road. Mary Cantrell turned pale at the sound. Old Jed went on sipping at his coffee and didn't even look up. Young Billy banged his own cup down on the table, then leaped across the room, threw open the door, and rushed outside. He was back in a couple of seconds, grinning from ear to ear.

"He's here!" he shouted. "Clayton Bannister is here!"

Then he rushed outside again to hold the great man's horse.

"That's mighty good rabbit stew, ma'am," Clayton Bannister said when he'd finished his second plateful. "I'm grateful for it."

"I'm grateful you're here," Mary Cantrell told him. She was clearing off the table. "I'm grateful to you all for coming out here to-night."

She took a seat across the table from Clayton Bannister and looked at him earnestly.

"I'm worried about what's going to happen tomorrow."

Clayton Bannister didn't let his gaze waver for a second. He just looked right back at her and the expression on his face didn't change a bit.

"Nothing to worry about, ma'am," he said.

The woman hesitated for a second then, and made believe she was brushing crumbs off the table, though she'd already made a good job of that. But after a little bit, she worked up her courage and spoke out what she was thinking.

"Mr. Bannister," she said, "please forgive me for sounding like this. It's just that I'm afraid of that man, that Siempre. He just rode into Two Trails and took over, shooting and killing, and nobody else but you has had the courage to even say a word. Nobody. Everybody in town has just pretended like nothing happened, and the longer they go on doing that, the longer they'll be before they can live with themselves and their own consciences. I don't blame a man for being afraid. Who wouldn't be afraid? You were the only one who spoke out—it's a mercy you're still alive—but you had to do it by yourself.

And you have to meet him again now, in the morning, and you're still alone."

"I'm not alone, ma'am," he told her quietly.

"But—"

"I have the three of you for company. No man can be alone when three people like yourselves are willing to stand by him."

Mary Cantrell hung her head at that and said real quiet, "Well, you can count on all the help you need, Mr. Bannister."

Then she raised her head and looked him right in the eye so he'd know she meant it. There was something like a transformation in her face too, like as if she all of a sudden was somebody else. Those dark eyes of hers were flashing like diamonds and she looked just about as set and determined as a body can look, man or woman.

"Do you know what you're going to do in the morning?" she asked him.

"I'm meeting him at the graveyard at dawn."

"And?"

"And we'll settle it."

"No, that's not what I mean. When you challenged him this afternoon, you fired your six shots, isn't that right?"

Bannister nodded and kept his eyes fixed right on hers.

"But you missed him."

A look of deep trouble, mixed with anger and puzzlement both, swept across the man's features like a dark cloud across the face of the moon. The others watched him closely, but only Mary Cantrell had the nerve to speak.

"When's the last time you fired six shots and missed?"

It was so quiet in that house, you could pretty near hear the ants crawling underneath it.

Clayton Bannister said nothing, only waited for her to go on and make her point.

When she spoke again, she'd controlled her nervousness and some of the edge was gone from her voice.

"That man, that Siempre, is something special. Something different. Seems to me you'd have to fight him in a special sort of way."

"I know that, ma'am," Bannister said quietly, his voice so soft the others could barely hear it. "And I've pretty near got it worked out."

Suddenly he rose from the table and the bulk of him seemed to fill the room.

"I'll just take some fresh air and then I'll be asking for your help."
And with that he strode across the room, opened the door, and disappeared into the night.

Clayton Bannister walked slowly down the path to the road and leaned against that white-painted fence. It was cold outside by then but he paid no attention to it. He had some thinking to do and he wanted to do it with no company except his old friends, the stars.

He was a man of few words when it came to talking with other folks, but his mind had been reeling with thoughts all afternoon and now the time had come to sort them out.

Never in his life had he seen the like of that gunfight. It wasn't just the open challenge from the man who called himself Forever, nor his opponent's lightning-fast draw, nor his deadly accurate aim, nor his ability to dodge bullets. Bannister had faced gunfighters before, and he was a gunfighter himself.

But he himself was different in one significant way from every gunfighter he'd ever had to face. He was still alive afterward to recall the battle.

But so was Siempre.

Out there in the main street of Two Trails, just the two of them facing each other, guns loaded and their lives hanging in the balance, that was something he understood. He'd been there before, and the thought of it didn't scare him. He knew he was no wonder-worker, too, and when his first bullet missed Siempre, he just naturally counted on the others. It wasn't the first time in a life of fighting that he'd missed with his first shot. But never once had he left a man standing up at the end. And he'd never faced a man who was fully his equal with a gun. Who was as fast as himself, or as brave. Or who looked so much like himself.

That was the heart of it. He had looked at Siempre's shape there in the road, with the brilliant sun beating down all around the two of them, and he'd been looking at the mirror image of himself. Same nerve. Same purpose. Same determination to win. Same confidence. Everything the same. Not just an equal match. No, there was more to it than that, one heck of a lot more.

Clayton Bannister had looked at Siempre, and he had seen himself.

And how was he going to fight that?

And how was he going to win?

He shifted his weight against the fence and raised his face to look at the stars.

How was he going to win against himself?

He had come here to Two Trails, to a place he'd never been before, a place that was farther west than he'd ever ridden before, to do two things. He wanted to get away from all the deaths he'd left in his path up till then. And he wanted to make peace with himself in preparation for his own death.

And now here were those two purposes come together in his path in the man who called himself Forever.

Well, then, he told himself, still looking at the stars, I'll just have to fight myself this time. And I've never lost a fight yet.

He turned sharply and his boots thudded on the path as he strode back up to the house.

Mary Cantrell, the boy, and the old man all studied his face anxiously as he came into the room.

"I'll need your help," he said, and they at once heard the renewed tone of determination in his voice. "I'll tell you what we need and then let's get to work."

The last few minutes before dawn is a beautiful time in the West. It's quieter then than any other time of the day. The creatures that do their business at night are just retiring from the field of battle, so to say, and the day crew hasn't come on duty yet. It's so quiet that even a man's innermost thoughts can sometimes seem loud as thunder in his head. It's a time when the whole world seems to be waiting, a time when anything at all can happen.

There's a gray light that comes up in the eastern sky just before dawn itself, and that's when the land starts to change. Rocks and trees and twisted mesquite stop being just flat shapes against the nighttime sky, and start moving with a life of their own. It's only their faint shadows, of course, sliding across the ground at their feet, but it's the only life they know. And it's a silent life.

And then the sun looks out past the horizon and the sky turns purple and red and then orange, and those shadows take shape and stretch out and slide fast along the ground.

It was just as the sky turned red that Clayton Bannister, riding at the head of his little party, saw the dark figure of Siempre waiting in the graveyard. He was sitting there on that big black horse, and looked like he might have been waiting there all night.

"So you come to your death on time," Siempre called as soon as they were within shouting distance.

Bannister let his horse walk slowly now, leading his party a little closer. He kept his head down as he rode and his hat was pulled low on his face.

They were near the unfenced edge of the graveyard and, even in the dim light of dawn, they could see the five fresh mounds of dirt that marked the graves of the men Siempre had killed. The earth had settled a little but the outlines were still clear.

"And you bring witnesses," Siempre called, and then he threw back his head and laughed.

Bannister reined in at the bottom of a shallow depression near the graveyard. There were a couple of stunted trees there and he stayed behind them, out of sight of the gunfighter. The three others brought their horses in close to his.

Bannister met Old Jed's eye and nodded, and the old man moved his horse forward over the rise. He rode to within a short distance of the stranger before he drew rein.

"Got a special request for you," he said.

Old Jed couldn't see Siempre's face, hidden by the dim light and the broad brim of his hat, but he knew those eyes were burning into him.

"You do," Siempre said. His voice showed no reaction at all.

"I do," Old Jed replied. His tone revealed only a hint of the defiance he felt for the gunfighter.

"And what gives you the right to come forward here, old man?"

"My age," Old Jed said, and he said it proudly.

The gunfighter made no reply, just sat that horse, as still as ever.

"Bannister says to dig your grave."

Siempre said nothing for a minute. All around them, shadows grew longer and the sky slowly turned a brighter red.

"Dig your grave and then stand in front of it. That way, when you go down, you'll go all the way."

"I won't be needing a grave."

"Bannister says to dig it."

"Then let him come and say it himself."

"No need," Old Jed told him flatly. "Me saying it's just the same as him saying it."

"He'll dig his own, then."

"Naturally."

At last—and it was almost a relief to the boy and the woman waiting in the hollow with Bannister—the rider in black burst into that harsh, ugly laugh of his again.

Old Jed urged his horse forward until he was alongside Siempre. He lifted a shovel from where it hung on his saddle horn and handed it across to the gunfighter.

"This spot'll do just fine," Jed said, then turned his horse and rode back slowly to where Bannister and the others were waiting.

Bannister, Billy Wagner, and Mary Cantrell had already dismounted. The horses' reins were thrown over a gnarled tree branch. Young Billy already had a shovel in his hand.

"We'll be done before him, too, I bet," the boy said, and boldly started up toward the top of the rise. Jed hitched his horse, took another shovel from Mary Cantrell's saddle, and went off to join him.

Siempre's laugh rang clearly in the morning silence when he saw the boy and the old man setting in to dig the grave for Clayton Bannister.

Bannister and Mary Cantrell ignored it.

He was sitting on the ground. Mary Cantrell was kneeling before him. She had poured a little water from a canteen onto the ground and made a small dark patch of mud. Now she was applying the mud with her fingertips to the left side of Bannister's face. She worked in silence, studying the effect critically.

Finally, she left off, sat back on her heels, and said, "I think it's right now."

Bannister said, "Feels right." He got to his feet and helped her up.

"You still have the hard part to do," she said softly.

"It'll be all right," he told her.

They were standing close together and Bannister could see those eyes of hers, those eyes that told him she had enough strength for herself and for him too, if he needed it.

They moved apart then and waited in silence until young Billy and Old Jed, the two of them sweating from their labors, came down from the top of the rise.

"Beat him to it," Billy said.

"He's just finishing up," Old Jed added.

Clayton Bannister looked over his shoulder at the eastern horizon where the sky was just starting to show a line of white.

"You ready with the rest?" he asked Jed.

Jed stepped over to his horse and took a stick of dynamite from his saddlebag.

"Got it right here," he said.

"You ready yourself?" Jed asked. "With the hand, I mean."

"I'm ready," Bannister told him.

"That outfit looks mighty fine," Billy Wagner said.

"You did a fine job, Billy," Mary Cantrell said to the boy. "It's exactly the right thing."

"Bannister!" Siempre called. "Come out and die! Grave's waiting for you!"

Bannister checked the eastern sky again.

"Go on, Jed," he said.

Old Jed Tree climbed to the top of the rise again, to where he could see Siempre. Then he slowly walked away, past the trees where the horses were tied. Billy unhitched the horses and he and Mary Cantrell moved in the same direction. They stayed on the lower ground, behind a curving hill, out of sight of Siempre.

"You set all the terms you want, Clayton Bannister!" Siempre called. "Just get on with it. It's time to die."

"Siempre!" Jed called. He had taken a position on a higher rise off to Siempre's left. "Here's how we'll do it. I'm going to light this here stick of dynamite and then I'm going to throw it away. When you hear the blast, you shoot. You stand in front of that grave you just dug and when you hear the blast, you fire."

"I'm ready," Siempre said. "Clayton Bannister, your time is up."

Clayton Bannister, still standing at the bottom of the hollow that hid him from Siempre, took a final moment to brush the trail dust from his clothes. Nothing could mar them or the plan would be spoiled. Young Billy Wagner could indeed be proud of the part he'd played in making the plan work. The boy had ridden in the night to Felix Hart's house behind the store in town, gotten him to open up, and find among his wares just the right clothing that would fit Bannister's big frame: new black boots, black trousers, belt, shirt, neckerchief, hat, and a holster designed to be worn on the left. Back at the house, Mary Cantrell had carefully stained the holster black from its natural worn brown, while Old Jed Tree had used all his skill and the patience of his years in blacking the butt of Bannister's gun.

The three others had done their parts. Now it was up to him to do his own.

He flexed the fingers of his left hand. He looked behind him once more at the eastern sky. The time was right.

Then he called out, "Siempre! I'm ready to kill you!"

He started up the rise to where his grave waited and where he could see the man he had to kill.

Siempre had earlier positioned himself at the top of another rise, figuring on having an advantage in shooting downward at Bannister. Behind him, the western sky was still dark and his own darkness blended with its color. His black hat still hid most of his face in shadow, but the growing light in the east now revealed the ugly, jagged scar, like a streak of lightning, that marked the left side of his face. His black boots were spread wide apart in the gunfighter's stance, directly in front of the open grave. His left hand hung poised and ready near the black handle of his gun.

Bannister appeared.

He was moving fast over the top of his rise, without giving the appearance of speed, and in a second or two he was in position. His black hat was pushed back to reveal in the rapidly growing light the scar that streaked across the left side of his face. His black clothes made him a dark figure, boldly outlined against the eastern sky. He planted his feet in front of the grave and took up his position, letting Siempre see his left hand poised by the handle of his gun.

Siempre crouched a little lower.

Bannister did the same.

"Ready!" Old Jed shouted. In the same instant, he touched a match to the dynamite and hurled it far away, aiming it toward the hollow where Bannister had waited before.

And a second later the explosion roared, and in the same instant the sun burst over the eastern horizon, filling the sky with light.

And in that very same instant too, the guns roared out, the two shots sounding almost as one.

Behind Bannister, the earth seemed to rise up in an explosion of smoke and dust, and the smoke and dust caught all the blinding light of the new sun. Bannister was outlined clearly against it for a fraction of a second, outlined there as he crouched, a figure all in black, left arm extended and his gun blazing away. And it seemed too that in that same instant, with the explosion of light behind him and his gun blazing like that, he hurled himself backward into the safety of his grave.

The sound of the blast and the roar of the guns rolled away across the empty land. The smoke disappeared and the dust slowly settled back to the earth.

Bannister climbed up out of the grave.

There was no sign of Siempre.

In the distance, the boy started to shout in triumph, but Old Jed's hand on his shoulder silenced him.

"Stay away," Bannister told the others.

Slowly he walked across the open space to where Siempre had stood to face him. He climbed the rise and stood at the top, looking down into the grave at what remained of the man who called himself Forever.

His bullet, as he knew already, had entered Siempre's heart.

He stood there a long time without saying a word.

Then at last he said, "Well, friend, now you know what it's like to come up against yourself. Slows you down just a bit."

A little distance off, young Billy Wagner had started hurrying forward again toward Bannister.

"I want to see his face!" the boy shouted.

"Stay there, son," Bannister told him, and Billy came to a halt.

"I want to see his face," Billy said again.

"No," Bannister said quietly, "you don't."

He bent forward and picked up the shovel Siempre had used earlier. Then he began filling in the grave of the man who called himself Forever.

7

Well, that's the end of the story, pretty near. The rest of it is just a matter of tidying up, so to speak.

The town of Two Trails went back to living a kind of normal life after that. Folks didn't talk too much, leastways not in public, about the way they'd acted when Siempre came in and took over. But things were different too. Folks worked harder, it seemed, and a lot of them started in to saving their money. And after a while some of them lit out for California, where they'd been heading in the first place before ever they laid eyes on Two Trails. Not all of them, of course, but some of them, and it kind of gave the others hope that they might get there someday themselves. Leastways, they had something to be thinking about, instead of just getting by from day to day.

Old Jed Tree stayed on in Two Trails a few years after that, but then one day he announced it was time for him to move on. He bought himself a horse and wagon and set out from there, heading west. Nobody knew where he was going, but they all figured, wherever that old fellow set his mind to be, that's where he'd end up. I reckon he got wherever he was going, too, and for all I know, he may still be alive. He had something in him, that old fellow did.

Mary Cantrell went on keeping her own private ways after that, but she must have been saving up her money like other folks, because one day she was gone too, just like Old Jed. Everybody was sorry she left, because she was the instrument, you might say, for saving the town of Two Trails. Nobody knew which direction she'd gone, because she left in the middle of the night, must have been, but folks reckoned she'd headed west like the others.

Clayton Bannister headed west, too. And when he went, he was riding on that black horse that had brought Siempre into town. He had never talked much about himself and he didn't tell anybody where he was going, and nobody ever heard of him again.

And young Billy Wagner?

Well, I reckon by now you've figured out that young Billy Wagner is me. I was there in Two Trails and I saw it all happening and I've told it as best I can just the way it was. I've had to imagine little bits of it, naturally, but it's all there and it's all true, pretty much.

I said at the beginning that Clayton Bannister is the hero of this story. He earned his name as the Man Who Killed Forever. The way I see it, that Bannister was a brave man when he first rode into Two Trails, and he was a braver man when he rode out. I reckon he's the bravest man I've ever seen.

But it's a funny thing, I can't help wondering sometimes how things might have been different if Mary Cantrell hadn't been a part of them. Seems to me, the end might have turned out otherwise from what it did. For one thing, maybe Clayton Bannister wouldn't have taken on Siempre like that. And maybe—I'm only wondering now— maybe he wouldn't have come out the winner in that particular showdown, either.

And there's another thing. Maybe not so many folks in Two Trails would have picked up afterward and continued on in the same direction they'd been going in the first place. Maybe I wouldn't have moved on westward myself when I got a little older. If I hadn't, I reckon I'd be a pretty different person from what I am today.

Well, it's just something to think about. There's no telling for sure, I guess.

Candlewyck

Chapter I

Never again can I return to Candlewyck. No one can. But Candlewyck, that strange and terrible house that burned so brightly for a brief while at the top of its beetling cliffs, shall remain as vivid in my memory as it was that first sunny day I saw it.

I was only eighteen then and, in the way of young girls, thought myself wise in the secrets of the world. My Aunt Beatrice, who accompanied me on that fateful voyage to my new home, never missed an opportunity of pointing out to me that, at eighteen, I still knew nothing really useful. I could always tell from the warm and loving look in her eyes that her heart felt differently, but she put on a stern face in the hope of setting me on a straight path against the rigors of adulthood.

And the hardest sort of rigors, I knew already, they were going to be. Aunt Beatrice never corrected me on that, for what else could they be for a girl in my situation? The world is not kind to orphans who confront it armed with nothing other than a pretty face (as I have been told), a patient disposition, and a fortunate facility for reading, writing, and a little music. My only other asset in all the world was dear sweet Aunt Beatrice herself, but she could offer little besides her love and good counsel, for she had sustained herself for many years on a meager allowance from a deceased elder brother, practicing the virtues of frugality and resignation. The only thing the dear old lady was not frugal with was her love for me, and I loved her equally in return. But love, I had already learned, put no bread upon the table.

In order to find a position, I had answered many of the advertise-

ments for companions and governesses in the newspapers, ignoring
only those that Aunt Beatrice deemed, for reasons that seemed im-
perative to her but often undefined to me, unsuitable. But there was
still a sufficiency in what my aunt called the "possibly suitable"
category, and I used my best hand in addressing letters to each of
them.

I fretted terribly during this period, because I knew I was a burden
to dear Aunt Beatrice. She, of course, said nothing, but I could see
the sadness and the worry in her lined old face each time she took up
her purse to go to market.

And then one day my hopes were answered.

The post had brought many letters but they had contained nothing
other than the discouraging information that the position I sought
was already filled. But the final letter, I knew at once, would be
different. Perhaps it was the fine quality of the paper or the bulkiness
of the envelope—"It contains directions and a map!" I told myself,
scarcely daring to breathe—or the bold masculine hand that had
inscribed the address, but I knew, from the very instant I first looked
upon it, that my fortunes were about to change at last.

I called urgently to Aunt Beatrice and she came in from the garden at once. We opened the envelope, extracted its contents, and read
the letter together.

"Dear Amanda Rutherford,"—the letter began—"I have read
with pleasure your expression of desire for the position of lady's
companion in my household. I have examined your qualifications, as
set forth in your letter, and find them quite satisfactory. If you will
have it, the position is yours. Please arrive by the ten o'clock train on
the eighteenth. My man will meet you at the station and bring you to
Candlewyck. (Signed) Geoffrey Paget-Poole."

"Oh, Aunt Beatrice," I cried when we had read the letter, "I have
found a position at last!"

Aunt Beatrice did not seem to share my joy, for she was frowning
at the letter she now held in her hand.

"It is not right," she said. "A gentleman should insist upon a
proper interview before engaging someone to enter his employ and
live in his household. And who is the lady to whom you shall be a
companion? The letter does not say." She sniffed, a sign, I knew, of
her severe disapproval. "I do not like it, Amanda. I do not like it at
all."

"Oh, Aunt Beatrice!" I cried. I had to press one hand across my bosom to still the fluttering of my heart, so fearful was I of losing my prospects in the very instant I thought them won at last. "I am sure everything is in order. It *must* be! What gentleman would write a letter such as this, offering a position in his home, if everything were not in order? Dear Aunt Beatrice, this is the opportunity we have both longed for so much!" In my excess of joy and hope, I threw my arms about the dear old thing and hugged her with all my might.

And then, with her gentle hand patting my shoulder, I realized what it was exactly that troubled her. Of course! It was not so much anxiety for my welfare—in that regard, she *must* be as pleased as I was myself—but rather her reaction was caused by a sudden realization that I would now be leaving her. She was distraught because our happy, companionable times together would shortly come to an abrupt end.

I drew back and held her at arm's length, forcing her to meet my gaze with her own. The dear lady's eyes were about to brim with tears which she was bravely holding back.

"Sweet Aunt Beatrice," I said gently. My voice threatened to betray my own emotion. "Dear Auntie, we both know this is for the best. Indeed, our circumstances in life make it a necessity, and nothing is served by either opposing or lamenting necessity. You have made that very point to me yourself many a time."

"My dear Amanda," she said. She took hold of both my hands and squeezed them. "Perhaps—" She had to pause and catch her breath before saying more. "Perhaps, after all, you are wise beyond your years. Forgive me for not giving you the credit you deserve. Oh, my child, I shall miss you terribly, but, yes, I suppose this is for the best. You know, dear, that I only want to see you placed in a position where you will be safe and secure from the troubles of the world."

"I know that, Auntie," I told her.

She released my hands and turned a little away from me to retrieve the letter from the table where she'd placed it. I saw the old look of strength and courage returning to her face. She read the letter once more, silently. I could see that she touched the paper and envelope with respect for their elegance and style.

"Yes," she said, looking at me again. "I suppose you are right, Amanda dear. I am an old woman and my ways of thinking are old too. Habits are different nowadays, less formal than they were in my time, and everything happens more quickly than it did in the past. Well, then, I'll say this. If the household itself has half the elegance of this letter, I shall consider it a happy stroke of Providence that you are so well placed. I shall miss you, of course, my child, but I shall rest easy every night with the thought that your future safety is assured."

"Oh, thank you, dear Auntie," I cried. Surely this was the highest act of love, wishing me well as I departed from her, and she so advanced in years. "I shall write to you every week, pages and pages," I promised her fervently. "And I shall tell you everything that is happening to me, absolutely everything!"

"Yes, child," she said, "and I shall look forward to each of your letters. And I shall pray God every day that you have only good news to relate."

But I could hardly hear those words of hers, so loud was the ringing of joy in my thoughts and the beating of my heart. At last, everything was working out just as I had so long hoped and prayed. Aunt Beatrice, while deprived of my company, would be relieved of the expense of keeping me and could live out her remaining years without worry. And I myself had a respectable position as lady's companion in a fine household where my needs would be taken care of and my future secure.

My fondest dreams had come true! No danger could possibly lie before me now!

Chapter II

A flood of emotions coursed through my mind as the train carried me ever closer to my destination that morning. Aunt Beatrice sat beside me. Although I had implored her to save the price of her fare, the dear lady had insisted on accompanying me as far as the station where Mr. Paget-Poole's man was to collect me. Part of me was touched by her love and care, yet another part of me—the bolder, more reckless, more forward-looking part—wished for the thrill of embarking alone in the world to have begun with the departure of the train, rather than its arrival. I was a woman now, whatever my years, and on my own. I had already, upon awakening that morning, begun to glimpse the serenity of adulthood for which I had so long yearned, mixed though it was with an undeniable fear of being alone in the world.

All the while the train rocked and swayed and carried us forward, I forced myself to sit still, like a proper lady, and to compose my thoughts for the adventure that lay ahead. In my mind's eye, I could picture my arrival.

The train would slow and come to a rattling halt. The porter would swing my one small case to the platform. Aunt Beatrice and I would embrace—she was taking advantage of the journey to visit a friend who had retired to a cottage farther along the coast—and I should step down to the platform, a woman on her own in the world at last. I should be calm and composed. No sooner than I had set foot upon the platform, with the train already hooting behind me, than a handsomely liveried servant would materialize before me. "Miss Rutherford?" he would enquire politely. I would bow my head briefly in acknowledgment. "Mr. Paget-Poole will be pleased to learn of your arrival," the man would say. "Won't you please come with me?" And he would sweep up my case and conduct me outside the station to a gleaming carriage drawn by a pair of perfectly matched and exquisitely groomed horses. This servant would be so handsomely turned out and so elegantly uniformed as nearly to rival his master. In time, so I imagined, the servant would fall in love with me and ask for my hand. Having put by his wages for some years already, he would now be in a position to take a wife, to purchase the modest little seaside hotel he had long dreamt of and at once install me as its mistress. We would cater only to persons of gentle background, and Aunt Beatrice should have the very best room, the corner one with the most splendid view of the sea, whenever she chose to visit.

I was happily lost in this dream of the future when the train clattered over a series of points and began to slow. My eyes sprang open and I stared out the window. Although the budding trees and springtime flowers were identical to those at home, I might have been transported to another country. I saw a road but did not know where it went or whence it came. At home, I knew every road and every lane. I saw a farmhouse but did not know the name of the family that lived within. Ahead I could make out a tiny village, but of course recognized none of the shops. I was, for the very first time in my life, in a wholly new and strange world. I drew in a very deep breath and let it out slowly. My adventure was about to begin!

Chapter III

Since both of us wished to avoid any public display of female emotion, my parting with Aunt Beatrice was brief, prolonged only by her renewed plea that I write her a letter regularly every week and my own fervent pledge to do so.

Just as I had imagined, the train porter had swung my case to the platform. I followed it down myself and instantly heard the train hoot behind me. Amid great clouds of white steam, it lurched once and then rapidly gained speed and disappeared behind a line of trees round a bend farther down the line.

Not a soul had descended from the train with me. There was no one in sight on the platform or in the vicinity of the station, and judging from the tightly shuttered booking office, there was no stationmaster on duty. And there was no servant, handsome or otherwise, to greet me politely and convey me to Candlewyck.

At last I had arrived in the wide world itself, as I had so often dreamed of doing. In contrast to my dream, however, I was utterly alone.

I took another deep breath—Aunt Beatrice had counseled that deep breaths worked wonders for calming the nerves in time of crisis —and looked about me.

The station itself was small and appeared to be a short distance from the village itself. There were no amenities of any sort to be seen, and no prospect of any. The dusty road that passed the station was deserted. What was I to do? I could carry my small case a short distance, if I had to—I was determined to be resourceful and self-reliant, as necessitated by my station in life—but I knew the limits of my physical strength would soon be reached. I scanned the platform for a bench, thinking I would wait a reasonable time for someone to collect me, but there was none in sight. I could not forbear allowing a sigh of disappointment—at least!—to escape me.

I gripped my case in both hands and struggled with it to the opposite side of the platform, beside the small stationhouse, and then seated myself, with as much delicacy as I could muster, on the edge of the platform. I composed my face as best I could to appear calm, but inside I was in a turmoil. Suppose this were the wrong station, the wrong date, the wrong time! Suppose Mr. Paget-Poole had received an enquiry from someone whose recommendations far surpassed my own poor ones, and he had decided not to engage me after all. The possibilities running through my thoughts were endlessly varied and endlessly frightening.

It was in this state and posture of barely concealed worry that I was collected at last by Mr. Paget-Poole's representative, although it is a concession to Christian charity to use such a word in describing the creature that suddenly loomed beside me, casting his shadow across my face and blocking, so it seemed, the very warmth of the sun.

How can I describe him and yet not seem to chastise the Deity in whose image all human beings are made?

He seemed, first, to have been the victim of some dreadful accident, perhaps a railroad disaster, in which, perhaps, a carriage had fallen across his back, for I at once perceived that his spine was bent almost in two and twisted painfully to one side. The posture thus forced upon the poor creature caused him always to be looking up and from the side at everyone about him. And his face! The left side of it was stained a bright and lurid—that is the only word—purple, whether as the result of some unimaginable mishap or as a mark from birth, I could not tell. As if recognizing the repulsive countenance he saw reflected in the eyes of all those who gazed upon him for the first time, his mouth was twisted in a hideous rictus of pain, and his knotty fingers were curled into spiny claws. He seemed almost to shrink in upon himself, so twisted was he, as if he would hide himself away from the sight of healthy and normal human beings.

His shadow took me by surprise, but as I was half expecting someone at any moment, I did not start as violently as I might have done. Even so, I could not repress a cry of, "Oh!"

The creature made some unintelligible sound.

Could this be the real-life version of the handsome servant I had imagined? Endeavoring to be polite, I said, "I'm sorry?"

"Candlewyck," he said, although the effort at clarity cost him dearly. It could not be easy to make oneself understood in society with that twisted mouth.

"Candlewyck!" I said eagerly, with more warmth than I felt inside. "Yes! You must be from Mr. Paget-Poole!" I realized at once that I was in danger of gabbling on in an attempt to spare him the effort of speech.

"Yar!" he growled, and his head sank even lower toward the ground—very like, it struck me at once, a dog that expects to be punished at every turn.

"Well, then!" I said quickly, covering my confusion with what I hoped was a businesslike and mature attitude. "I have only the one case, there, so we can be off straightaway."

With a crablike motion, as I have seen it described, the creature moved sideways and hooked the handle of my bag with one of his claws, then scuttled, with more speed than I would have thought possible for one so misshapen, toward the road that passed the station.

With considerable misgivings that I struggled to contain, I followed along behind him.

Outside the station, and concealed from where I had been sitting, was a small carriage with a single horse dozing in the traces. Neither vehicle nor beast was in any way prepossessing, but at least neither shared the lowly state of the driver.

I saw my bag tossed lightly inside, and I followed it myself with only a little greater dignity.

Now, however, seated properly and with my transportation assured, I felt a trifle bolder and ventured to speak again.

"My name is Amanda Rutherford," I said.

The man, who had not yet mounted to his seat at the front of the carriage, cocked his head and looked up at me with bloodshot eyes. A rope of saliva dripped from the lower corner of his mouth, and I disciplined my eyes to avoid staring at it.

I cleared my throat and began again. "I am Miss Rutherford, and I am to be lady's companion in the home of Mr. Paget-Poole."

The man shook his head as a horse or donkey might, but said nothing.

"And what is your name?" I asked.

He seemed to be considering, as if perhaps I could not be trusted with such intimate information. Then he made a sound which I interpreted to be a clearing of the throat and continued looking up at me.

"Sorry?" I said.

He cleared his throat again, whereupon I realized that this guttural and unpleasant sound was, in fact, his name.

I hesitated to attempt a repetition of the sound, but there was nothing for it.

"Crickback? Is that it?"

"Crickback!" the creature said.

Sometimes, when we are terribly frightened, we find strengths within ourselves never previously utilized. I managed my warmest smile.

"Well, then, Crickback," I said, "I suppose we should be on our way. I'm very eager to see Candlewyck and meet Mr. Paget-Poole."

Without lowering his eyes from mine, the creature muttered something indecipherable. Then, with an agility that surprised me, he climbed up to his seat in the front. A moment later, the carriage was moving slowly along the road.

As we left the shadow of the station behind us, I tried to puzzle out what it was Crickback had said. It was only some twenty minutes later, as I was still repeating the sound silently to myself, that I realized his words had been, "Candlewyck means death."

But it was too late for me to contemplate further the meaning of this, for suddenly, as the carriage rounded a sharp turn in the road, I saw a massive shape, bathed in sunlight but seemingly dark against the brilliance of the blue sea beyond it, that could only be Candlewyck itself—Candlewyck, that would henceforth be my home!

Chapter IV

Candlewyck was set upon the very brow of the cliffs above the sea. Later I learned that these cliffs are the highest on that entire part of England's southern coast, and Candlewyck was set upon the very highest of them.

It was a massive house, many-windowed, turreted and towered, its walls constructed of the same gray stone that formed the mighty cliffs themselves. It seemed, almost, as if it rose out of the earth of its own volition, borne up by a will derived from its own strength, offering a challenge to the world, to the hills behind it, to the cliffs before it, to the sea and to the sky. It took my breath away just to look upon it.

Rosebushes, fallen into decay, struggled for life against the walls. A broad stone terrace fronted the house and a driveway for carriages curved in toward the covered portico of the door. In front of the terrace a greensward, somewhat ragged in appearance, sloped downward to the very edge of the precipice. Below the precipice was only the sea. I could hear it booming against the tumbled rocks at the base of the cliff. Some trick of the rock formations or the cliffs themselves magnified the sound and carried it upward, like a wave that covered the house. I soon learned that this roaring and crashing of the sea was a steady companion of life at Candlewyck, an invisible presence in all the rooms, as constant as the anxious beating of my own heart.

But for the moment, at least, I was not frightened. At least, I was too overcome by a welter of emotions to feel any one emotion in particular.

The sun was shining brightly, a gentle breeze from the sea was freshening the air, and the house in which I was to live henceforth was even grander than I could have imagined. Each bit of information I took in only whetted my appetite for more. When would I meet my employer? When would I meet the lady to whom I was to be companion? Who would she be? Would we become dear friends?

What were to be my duties? Which was to be my room? The questions swirled in my head, nearly making me dizzy.

And then I saw him. There, standing in the doorway beneath the portico, was a tall and finely made man of middle years. His stance, the way one hand rested casually on the frame of the door, indeed everything about him, proclaimed him the master of Candlewyck. Here at last was Mr. Paget-Poole, my employer!

Crickback slowed the carriage and brought it to a halt beneath the portico. Before it had even stopped completely, Mr. Paget-Poole, smiling, stepped forward and extended a carefully manicured hand to help me down. I was immediately struck by this, for he was treating me as if I were a guest in his house, or a member of the family itself, rather than merely the newest of his servants. I could not help myself; I blushed.

"Miss Rutherford, of course," he said when I stood before him.

I knew at once he was both the handsomest and most charming man in all the world. His dark suit was cut perfectly to flatter his tall and well-kept figure. His boots sparkled. A touch of gray at the temples and dark moustaches added dignity to his face, which was otherwise craggy and eloquent of decades spent in the world at large. His eyes were dark and did not, somehow, mirror that smile that softened his mouth, and this immediately struck me as a telling detail. Those eyes, dark and troubled and mysterious, had no doubt witnessed all the vicissitudes and mysteries of life.

I curtsied. "I am very pleased to be here," I said.

Still smiling, he inclined his head slightly. "I trust your journey was a pleasant one?" His voice was deep and sonorous, the rhythms of his speech suggesting generations of breeding and a lifetime of culture.

"Oh, yes, sir, very pleasant."

"Good," he said. "But I am certain you must be tired."

He was silent for a moment and seemed to be studying my face intently. Then he, so it appeared, drew himself back from a sudden reverie.

"Please do come in, Miss Rutherford. We must see you settled comfortably." He stepped back toward the open doorway. I saw him make a peremptory gesture in the direction of Crickback who, during this exchange, had kept himself at a little distance. Now he scuttled forward, my bag clutched in one knotted hand.

"You know where to put it," said the master, and Crickback hurried into the darkness within, taking care not to brush against his employer.

"Come along," said Mr. Paget-Poole.

I stepped forward and set foot for the first time within the walls of Candlewyck.

In contrast to the brilliant sunshine outdoors, all was darkness within. I followed my employer across the width of the entrance hall and up the broad curving stairs that faced the door. My room, it appeared was to be on the topmost floor and—could it be true!—at the front of the house, facing the sea.

"Here you are, my dear," said Mr. Paget-Poole. He threw open a door on our right, then stood aside for me to enter. This was a courtesy I hardly thought my position warranted, but I was thrilled nonetheless.

The room already felt like home. Crickback—I already felt accustomed to the name—had hurried ahead and deposited my case just inside the door. Before me was a small sitting room with a pretty fireplace and, through an open door on my left, I glimpsed a bedroom. Two rooms of my own! The shutters on the windows were drawn, but I could see a sliver of light around the edges and I could hear the pounding of the sea. I felt I needed nothing more to ensure my perfect happiness!

"I trust everything is satisfactory?" asked my employer.

"Oh, yes!" I cried, then quickly blushed to see his smile widen at my girlish happiness.

"But I am eager to meet the lady for whom I am to be companion," I added quickly. Certainly I did not want him to think I was unmindful of my duties.

"Oh, yes," he said, and I thought his smile faded a little as he spoke. "You shall, my dear, you shall. There is all the time in the world for that, my dear, I assure you, all the time in the world. For now, I would be pleased to know that you are resting from your travels until it is time for tea. Please join us then."

And with that, he stepped out of the doorway and closed the door firmly behind him.

I was alone at last in my own little precinct within the walls of Candlewyck. I could hardly wait to begin exploring! With a little cry, I rushed across to the windows and threw open the sashes and shutters. The room was filled at once with sunshine, salty air, and the sound of the crashing sea. There were three windows in all—for, with the daylight flooding in, the room was even larger than I had at first thought—and I opened the others quickly. Then, filled with joy at my good fortune, I rushed into the adjoining bedroom and threw open the two windows there. I knew Aunt Beatrice would not have approved of so much fresh air being permitted within the house, but the light and the scent and sound of the sea filled me with an exhilaration I had scarcely ever known before.

I stared happily from the windows, comparing the view from each —although, of course, they differed not at all—and thinking them each and every one splendid. Finally, with a contented sigh, I carried my bag into the bedroom, set it on the bed, which was prettily made, and prepared to unpack my few belongings.

I spent some time at this, for, in my excitement, I kept rearranging things in the wardrobe, but at last I was done, my bag tucked away, and I felt that I had indeed taken up permanent residence here. Candlewyck was my home!

I lay down upon the bed, recklessly stretching myself out atop the counterpane, and happily closed my eyes to dream a little about the happy future that stretched endlessly before me. It was only then, with the room silent and my thoughts no longer racing, that I first heard the unmistakable sound of *anguished sobbing*.

Chapter V

"My Dearest Aunt Beatrice," I began a letter that night.

"I have not yet spent a night through at Candlewyck, and do not yet know what the days ahead may bring, so I have made a plan, a little promise to myself—no, dear Auntie, it is a *solemn vow*—that, each night before remembering you in my prayers and retiring, I will set down some lines to you while the impressions are still fresh and vivid in my thoughts. Then, once each week, I shall gather up the pages and send them off to you, and meanwhile shall have had the pleasure, as it will seem, of talking with you every evening. Oh, Auntie, I miss you so much!

"First, to allay the worries I know you are suffering on my behalf, I must tell you that Candlewyck is in every detail just as I imagined it to be, Mr. Paget-Poole is the very model of a proper and genteel employer, and the lady for whom I am to fill the role of companion is—"

But I had nothing further to write on that point, for, as I took myself upstairs on that first night in Candlewyck, the truth was that I remained still in ignorance of her identity.

Who was she? Wife? Daughter? Sister? An aging and infirm mother? I did not know, and my tentative enquiries to Mr. Paget-Poole had elicited no information whatsoever. His only response to my expressions of curiosity was to the effect that there was all the time in the world for that. When I enquired if the lady would be joining us for tea, and, later, if she would be coming down for the evening meal, my questions were ignored and brought forth from my employer only a further question about myself and my own background.

The meals were both prepared and served by Crickback, who evidently was the only servant in the house. I noticed then how pale he was, like a creature who never sees the sun. Indeed, he seemed at one with all the very darkest corners of Candlewyck. He moved with an unsteady shuffle, his head lowered as if to stare distrustfully at her feet, and the hands that clutched plates and trays were twisted with painfully enlarged knuckles. Mr. Paget-Poole hardly took notice of him and, when it came time to eat, applied himself to the food as if it had appeared on the table before him through the powers of magic.

To my surprise, I was invited to sit at the table with the master for the evening meal. I was relieved at this, for I could not imagine enjoying any meal taken in the kitchen in the company of the silent creature who presided there, however kind he might be in other respects, and was not a little alarmed at the prospect, as I assumed, of taking all my meals there in the future.

Despite my pleasant situation at the moment, sitting at the master's own table, I began to realize, bit by bit, that Candlewyck would take some growing accustomed to!

Afterward, I returned to my room no wiser than I had been when I left it.

And of course, still feeling myself very much the newcomer, I had said nothing about the sobbing.

I heard it again when I closed my door and turned to face my rooms. It had never stopped while I was away, I was quite certain.

It was female sobbing, interrupted by intervals of silence, then renewed as if the anguished person had been forced to stop only for lack of breath. My heart was rent by the sound.

I had earlier determined that it came from the room next to my bedroom, just on the other side of the wall, behind the wardrobe. As I had approached my door on my return, I had thought of continuing on down the passage and listening at the next door in line, perhaps even knocking at it to see if I could be of any assistance, but the strange manner of my employer, on the subject of the lady of the house, had discouraged me. Perhaps this was his beloved wife who was suffering the ravages of some dread disease. Perhaps—I prayed this was not the case!—there was *madness* in the family. Lacking permission and instruction, I feared to tread where I had not been invited.

Now, however, alone in my room where I could not be observed, I grew a little bolder and thought I would listen at the wall and perhaps gain a clue to the identity of my poor troubled neighbor in the next room.

But I learned nothing. The sounds continued but were no different than they had been. Several times I opened my lips to call softly, but, each time, I grew fearful and stopped myself. After a few minutes of this, I retreated into my sitting room and began composing a letter to Aunt Beatrice. But always I could hear the sobbing, and finally it drew me back to the wall.

The sound was the same as ever, a hoarse, dry sobbing that tore me through and through. No, I told myself, I cannot leave a fellow creature in such torment! Before my courage should leave me, I cried out, "Hello! Can I help you?"

The sobbing ceased abruptly. The only sound was the rapid beating of my heart and the rush of blood in my ears.

And then the sobbing began again. I could not be certain, but I thought that, if anything, it sounded even more anguished than it had before.

"Hello!" I called again. "Hello! I'll help you if I can!"

Again the sobbing ceased.

"Hello?" I said, my face pressed close against the wall.

Only silence greeted me, although I thought I could just hear a sound that might have been the creaking of a floorboard pressed by a stealthy or terrified foot. I held my breath.

And then, from the other side of the wall, a choking voice, racked with pain or misery or both, called softly, as if it dreaded to be detected, "Hello?"

My heart skipped a beat and for a moment I grew faint and the room swam about me.

"Yes!" I called, whispering as loudly as I dared. "I'm here. I'll help you if I can."

There was only silence.

"Can you hear me?"

Silence again, and then, faintly, "Yes."

I forced myself to draw in a deep breath.

"My name is Amanda Rutherford," I whispered, hoping my voice would carry through the wall without being heard elsewhere in the great house. "I have only just come to Candlewyck."

I could not be certain but I thought I heard the unseen voice repeat my name, "Amanda," in tones that seemed expressive of the deepest sorrow. Even so, I interpreted this response as a sign of encouragement and hurried on.

"Can I help you in any way?"

Each of my enquiries was greeted by a lengthy silence before any answer was returned.

"No one can help me," said the voice, sounding even fainter and more despairing than it had before.

"I shall try," I whispered. "I shall do my utmost."

Silence, only silence.

"What is your name?" I called.

After what seemed an age, the reply came back through the wall.

"I have no name."

What a dreadful thing for a human being to feel! Without even thinking of my words or moderating my voice, I cried out, "But you must!"

And at last the response came back.

"Names are for the living."

My heart nearly stopped within my breast to hear such words! Of what terrible fate could the speaker be a victim? What had befallen her to reduce her to such a state of despair?

And then another terrible thought—one I hardly dared permit myself to think—rushed in upon me. Could Mr. Paget-Poole, the master of Candlewyck, be responsible for this poor creature's condition? Could he be the instrument of her pain and terror? No, the idea was too terrible to countenance!

But even as I willed the thought away, it echoed in my brain and grew in substance. My employer was, after all, master of Candlewyck and all that it contained. Was it possible that a living creature be walled up within the house and he not know it? No. Was it possible that someone else was inflicting harm on my invisible neighbor and he not be aware? No.

And then I was forcibly struck by an even more terrifying thought. Was it possible that Mr. Paget-Poole had installed me in this very room merely by accident? And the undeniable answer was once again: No!

Was I to be a prisoner too?

I was drawn suddenly back from this horrifying train of thought by a trembling call from my neighbor.

"Are you still there? Amanda? Oh, please, answer me!"

"Yes!" I called at once. "Yes, I'm still here!"

"Oh!" was all I heard, followed by renewed sobbing which was quickly cut off.

"Tell me your name," I called. "Oh, do tell me your name!"

I waited, holding my breath. Even in my own acute fear, I knew that the poor victim on the other side of the wall must surely regain some strength and courage through the simple act of naming herself.

She made a sound then but her voice was too weak for me to hear.

"Again," I whispered. "Come closer to the wall." With a shudder, I suddenly wondered if some demon had placed her in chains or otherwise restrained her. Perhaps she *could not* come any closer. "Oh, please do say your name again."

"Mary." With my ear pressed tightly against the wall, which made me shiver with its coldness, I was able to make out the name amid a new round of yet more anguished sobbing. And then, more clearly, the poor thing's full name reached me through the barrier that separated us: "Mary Cantrell."

"Oh, Mary!" I was nearly sobbing myself, but struggled to keep

control. Now that I knew her name, the sufferer, although in all
other respects still a stranger to me, seemed as close as I imagined a
sister would have been. "Oh, Mary, let me help you. I shall do
everything in my power!"

Her reply to this came through to me more plainly than any of her
other words, and sent an even colder chill through my quaking heart.

"No!" she cried, more forcefully than she had spoken at any time
before. "No! You cannot remain here! Leave me! Go away! Oh, do go
away while you can! Go away from Candlewyck this very hour and
save yourself!"

I heard nothing more from Mary Cantrell that night.

Chapter VI

Oh, the thoughts that assailed me as I lay there in the dark on my
first night at Candlewyck!

The house and the future that had beckoned so invitingly, with
such warm and cozy promise, only a dozen hours before, now
seemed filled with monstrous shapes that threatened from every
point of the compass. Candlewyck itself, the first sunny sight of
which had filled my fluttering heart with so much joy that very
morning, now seemed to me little better than a foul and dank prison.
Mr. Paget-Poole, he of the elegant clothes and charming manners, a
man of grace and courtesy, had now been transformed in my
thoughts to a demon of unspeakable evil.

I tossed from side to side in my bed, a bed that now gave me none
of the repose and comfort it had earlier promised, and struggled
against such thoughts. But there was no winning against them. I
brought to bear on them every shred of Christian charity and every
possible explanation I could muster—The woman next door was
mad! I myself was mad!—but none prevailed. Mr. Paget-Poole was a
monster of evil and Candlewyck *a very nest of the devil!*

My thoughts were in no way eased by the incessant pounding of
the sea at the base of the cliffs. I had closed the windows tightly to
shut out the damp vapors of the night and the constant roar of the

surf, but it was to no avail. The dampness crept in at every crevice, it seemed, and chilled me through and through, and the hammering of the sea against the rocks rivaled the furious beating of my own heart, stirring it on to double and triple its natural speed. Several times I had to press my hand to my mouth to keep from crying out.

And then suddenly I sat bolt upright on the bed. I saw again in vivid detail the twisted form of Crickback, the servant. (How prophetic, I thought now, was that, my first introduction to Candlewyck!) No longer did he appear the sad victim of some disfiguring accident. Oh, no—rather he seemed now the very embodiment of evil, his body racked by a justly vengeful God as punishment for his *hideous sins.*

And I heard once again the guttural, animal-like mutterings of the creature, and his words, which I had barely been able to decipher earlier and which had left my distracted thoughts in less time than it had taken him to speak them, came back to me with the clarity of a voice speaking directly in my ear.

"Candlewyck means death!" the creature had said.

Now, huddled on my bed, alone in the night—the first night of my life spent in a house where no one loved me!—and having already learned one terrible secret about Candlewyck, I had no choice but to believe the awful truth of the creature's misshapen words. Candlewyck meant death indeed, and I could not help but think that it meant it for me.

Thus passed my first night in that evil house.

Chapter VII

It is a universal truth among humankind that nothing looks so dark and dreadful in the new-born light of dawn as it did in the dead of night. I awakened—if I may truly say so, for I had hardly been to sleep at all—with a hint of crimson just peeking through the slits of the shutters, and, despite my fright of only a few hours before, it was several seconds before I remembered the terrible fright I had suffered in that very room.

Could I have imagined it? Could I have dreamt it? Perhaps it was merely the product of a fevered imagination, set in motion by the unaccustomed strangeness of travel and taking up residence in a house I had never seen before. Perhaps, in truth, it was nothing more than a product of the girlish terrors of setting out alone in life with nothing to rely on but my own wits and meager resources.

I climbed stealthily from the bed, half expecting at any moment to hear the sobbing that I had heard before. The only sound was my own breathing, the whisper of the bedclothes as I pushed them back, and then the faint groan of the ancient floorboards as I stood upright beside the bed. There was no other sound. I might have been alone in the house. Indeed, I might have been utterly alone in the world.

Treading as lightly as I could, I moved close to the spot on the wall where I remembered crouching fearfully the night before. I held my breath and pressed my ear to the wall. Not a sound. I shifted my position and listened again. Nothing.

I straightened up and drew my robe around my shoulders.

What a silly thing I was, what a silly, foolish girl! To dream such fantasies. Why, it had only been a nightmare, nothing more, my troubled imagination running rampant. I blushed at my own foolishness as I crossed to the nearer window and threw open the sash and then the shutters.

Directly below me was the stone terrace, and beyond that, the green lawn that sloped downward to the edge of the cliff. As I looked out, I thought there might be some danger there, the edge of the cliff being unfenced and unprotected. But this was the only disturbing thought that troubled me, for all the world seemed a warm and peaceful place. Breezes touched my face, birds sang their cheery songs, and even the pounding of the sea against the cliff seemed somehow reassuring, a reminder that the world was a fine and wonderful place.

The absolute silence of the house convinced me that I was the first to stir on this fine morning. I immediately resolved to dress at once and slip out, before the rest of the household was astir, and explore a bit on my own. It seemed, to part of my mind, an audacious plan, but the pink sky in the east and the freshness of the air would not be denied. I almost laughed with sheer pleasure as I dressed hurriedly and tied the strings of my bonnet beneath my chin.

I had not had a proper tour of the house the day before. I assumed there were back stairs for the use of servants—did not great houses such as this always have back stairs?—but I did not know where they might be. Cautiously I slipped out of my room and, on tiptoe, hoping the old staircase would not betray me, crept down the stairs to the foyer. I had a moment's panic when the latch on the front door would not yield to me, but then it opened and I was outside.

What a prospect lay before me! Tall and ancient oak trees ringed the house on three sides, but none grew so close as to block the sunlight. Before the house, almost seeming to float there for Candlewyck's special delight, was the sea. It was gray now in the first light of day, reddened by the rising sun in the east, and not as blue as it would be later on, but to me it seemed the prettiest view of the sea I had ever enjoyed. Flowers scented the air. A breeze stirred the grass as it rippled in luxuriant waves. I hugged myself for sheer pleasure.

With my heart racing in my chest, I crossed the terrace and stepped onto the springy surface of the lawn. I felt suddenly bold, bolder than I'd ever felt before, bold enough even to dare the very edge of the cliff.

Some ten feet, as I imagined, from the edge of the precipice, I stopped and turned to look back at Candlewyck. I had only ever seen engravings of great houses such as this. Never had I dreamed that I should one day live within the walls of such a house. The sun was just coming above the horizon now and its rays, as I watched, touched the glass of the dozens of windows and set them dancing with color and brilliance. Every window seemed a face and every face seemed to be smiling upon me, laughing with delight. Even the dark stone of the house took on a friendly aspect, as if it meant to promise only solidity, patience, and everlasting safety.

I turned back to the sea and, holding my breath, startled by my own nerve and sense of adventure, took three steps closer to the edge. The sea roared up at me. I longed to see the waves and the curling foam I imagined to be breaking over the rocks, but this was invisible to me from where I stood. I edged a little closer. With each step I took, the sea seemed to roar yet more loudly. I took another step, and then another.

I stood now within two feet of the edge. Never before had I been in such a position. I felt the reassuring solidity of the ground beneath my feet, and, at the same time, I felt that I floated on the very air, that a breeze only a little more forceful than the last one might carry me off from the land and waft me out across the sea.

I looked down and, far below me, saw the waves. They boiled and curled with white foam as they swept in powerfully and crashed against the rocks and boulders tumbled at the foot of the cliffs. A narrow stand of gravel stretched along the very base of the cliff. Oh, I thought, what must it be like to stand there, with the sea pounding in relentlessly before one, and a hundred feet, at least, of solid rock at one's back.

Keeping my eyes, for safety's sake, on the edge of the cliff, I moved a little distance to my left. The cliff, I could see, was nearly sheer, but to the left it began to slope a little as it approached the stand of trees on that side. Surely it was too steep to support a footpath. I must explore the cliff, I told myself, as opportunity offered, and see if I could find a way down to that narrow bit of strand. I was fully convinced already that Candlewyck occupied the most beautiful headland on all the coast of England, and I must learn every inch of it before I could be satisfied.

I halted. Ahead of me, to the left along the cliff, a fissure stretched back from the edge, as if a giant axe had once, long ago, been driven into the stone and torn out a wedge. I stepped a little closer. Yes, a wide V cut deeply into the cliff. The raw wound—for so it seemed—was a scatter of rocks, nearly free of vegetation.

Immediately I wondered if it might be possible to make one's way down by this means. I studied the tumble of rocks in the V. What was that? A rock just below the level of the lawn looked as if it might have been placed there as a step, or perhaps lucky chance had just settled it that way. And then, just a little below it, I saw another rock that had a similarly flat surface. Could this be a gigantic stairway? Was that possible? Even though the idea might suit my girlish fancy for wild exploration, what need could there be for the trouble such a project would have taken?

When I straightened up from studying the rocks, I was suddenly blinded by the brilliance of the dawning sun. I began to wonder about the time. I should not want Mr. Paget-Poole to think me a silly and flighty young thing—although I very probably was exactly that! —on the very first morning I spent at Candlewyck. And no doubt he was by now satisfied with me after our conversations the day before, and would be eager to introduce me to the lady for whom I was to be companion. My mind whirled with all the changes and surprises of the last twenty-four hours.

I drew another deep breath of fresh morning air into my lungs. A new day lay before me! At Candlewyck, my home!

Bursting with excited resolve, I turned quickly from the sea and started briskly up the slope toward the house.

The very next thing I knew, I was clinging for dear life to the edge of the cliff and the hideous face of Crickback was *leering down at me!*

Chapter VIII

I shall never, so long as it pleases God to let me live, forget the terror I felt in that awful moment.

I hung there at the edge of the void, clinging desperately by my fingertips, the wind driven from my lungs by sudden fright. Far below me were the savage rocks that only a moment earlier had appeared so picturesque. Now they waited eagerly, as I thought, to smash my fragile body when I fell, as I was convinced I must. And there were the savage waves—Oh, how loud and vicious sounded their hungry roaring in my ears!—waiting in their turn to devour the broken bits left by the rocks. And beneath my fingers was only the slippery grass, wet with the dew of morning, affording no purchase to my straining and clawing fingertips. With every passing second, every heave of my straining and aching body, I felt myself slip closer and closer to the bloody fate that awaited me below.

And above! Crickback's face moved closer to me with a dreamlike slowness. Oh, that hideously contorted face, saliva running from one corner of the mouth and dripping from the chin. A strand of it touched the back of my hand as I clutched desperately at the grass, and I nearly shook it to fling away the revolting fluid.

He had pushed me! I knew it! "Candlewyck means death!" he had said to me on my arrival. I had thought his words demented prattling and had paid them little heed. But they had not been mere prattling. Rather, they were a promise, and now he meant to make good on his threat. Oh, what had I done to deserve such an end?

Even in my extremity of terror, I thought then of dear Aunt Beatrice and the pain she would suffer on learning of my fate. I prayed fervently that she would never have to look upon the broken remains of my body, if, that is, it could be recovered from the depths of the sea, which would no doubt be jealous of its prize and reluctant to give it up. Perhaps I thought, overwhelmed by helplessness, that would be best in the end, for the sight would surely kill the dear old lady.

Crickback's face dropped closer to my own. He was on his knees. Those terrible gnarled hands of his reached out to my arms. He will finish the job now, I thought, pull my hands free of the earth and send me crashing to the rocks below.

But that was not the case. The creature was gabbling madly but I could not make out a single word he said. Even so, I knew that those hands closed like vises around my arms.

Crickback was stretched out now upon the earth—insofar as such a twisted and deformed creature could be said to stretch out upon anything—and he was pulling me back from the edge!

Tears of relief streamed down my face. He was saving me, not murdering me! I felt my shivering body pulled upward, while the waves below seemed to hurl themselves against the rocks with renewed fury.

I looked pleadingly up into the face of Crickback. I wanted to cry out *Oh, save me, save me!* but no words would form in my throat. Then I felt myself rise above the edge of the cliff.

I have often heard that our loving Lord and Maker compensates some people for losses by blessing them with other graces. This was the case with Crickback, for he was gifted with prodigious strength. And as he pulled me at last to safety and stretched me out on the dear, solid earth, he was transformed before me. No longer was he a hideous misshapen creature, as I had ungenerously seen him before, but an angel of mercy, radiant with the grace of God Who had sent him to my rescue. Never again should I avert my eyes from his countenance and regard him as less than human. Crickback had saved my life!

I lay on the ground, panting for air, struggling to form words of gratitude but still unable to do so. The ground beneath me seemed to lift me up and support my weight with blessed ease.

I opened my eyes—perhaps it had taken me only seconds but it seemed like ages—and gazed upon my savior. I opened my lips to thank him but stopped in the same instant, for graven on his face was a look of the sheerest terror!

He was looking toward the house. My gaze instantly followed his own and I saw Mr. Paget-Poole rushing toward us across the lawn. His face was red, his eyes blazing, and his whole countenance suffused with the purest expression of *unadulterated hatred* I had ever witnessed in my life!

Chapter IX

There was no mistaking it. Mr. Paget-Poole was in a rage that terrified me nearly as much as my recent brush with death.

"Fool!" he shouted as he drew near us. He came to a halt and stood above us, breathing heavily. A muscle in his jaw and another near his left eye twitched convulsively. A thick, dark vein throbbed at his temple. His race across the lawn had disarranged his hair and he had, in every respect, the look of a madman newly escaped from his asylum.

"Fool!" he cried again. "Hideous brute!" His eyes wild with rage, he made a vicious swipe at poor Crickback, who cringed and whimpered at my side.

I struggled upright from the ground.

"Oh, please," I cried. Boldly—I do not know whence came my nerve, except from a consciousness of injustice being done—I thrust myself between them. "Please, sir, do not strike him. It was not his fault. He saved me. It is by his hand that I stand before you now!"

My employer looked from one to the other of us repeatedly, as if he knew not where to fling his sharpest arrows. I repeated my plea in behalf of Crickback as strenuously as I could, and after some minutes Mr. Paget-Poole grew a little calmer. The red of his face declined to an agitated pink and he brushed the disarrayed hair back from his forehead. It took a visible effort for him to steady his impassioned breathing, but at last he was able to speak.

"I see," he said. "Yes, of course, I see." Despite his words, something troubled me about the way in which he said them. "I thought it was this brute"—he cast a look of utter loathing and disgust at poor Crickback—"who tripped you. Or worse." He turned on his pathetically cringing servant. "You!" he snapped. "Get out of my sight!"

Crickback only half rose from the ground and scuttled as quickly as he could across the lawn.

"My dear," Mr. Paget-Poole said, turning to me and placing a supporting hand beneath my elbow. "My dear child, please forgive my rough language. I would never be moved to speak thus except by fear for your well-being. Poor thing, you've had a terrible fright. Here, let me help you to the house."

With Mr. Paget-Poole supporting me with a firm hand, I made my way across the lawn, yearning for the solitary comfort of my room until I should collect myself and regain a little of my strength. But now, after the fright I had suffered, and after the savagery of Mr. Paget-Poole's appearance on the scene, to make no mention of the fact that I was made very distrustful by the tone of voice in which he spoke, I could not prevent the tears from springing to my eyes. I sobbed aloud.

The instant I made a sound, I felt my employer stiffen at my side. In my weakened state, this served only to terrify me further, although for what reasons I could not say, and I burst openly into tears. Oh, I deplored the womanly weakness in me that made me do it, but I could not help myself. I cried and cried, trying to choke back the sobs but failing, and the burning tears streamed copiously down my face.

As I stumbled across the lawn toward the entrance of the house, I chanced to look up. I do not know why I did so, unless I was seeking my own windows for the comfort they would promise. But it was not a comforting sight that met my yearning, tear-blurred gaze.

At a window in the room on the topmost floor, just next to mine, the very room from which had issued the anguished sobbing of the night before, I saw the pale and terrified face of a girl my own age. She drew back fearfully as our eyes met, but not before we had exchanged a look that was eloquent of our *mutual terror!*

Chapter X

As he had on my arrival the day before, Mr. Paget-Poole himself conducted me to my rooms. I noticed that he did not actually enter the sitting room but remained in the doorway, almost as if he wished not to intrude on my distracted state. Part of me was willing—nay, eager—to count this as the natural delicacy of a gentleman, but a more forceful part of me insisted that Mr. Paget-Poole was on no account to be trusted.

I thanked him as courteously as I could manage, although I was still trembling from head to foot.

"Rest, my dear," he said softly. "Rest." I saw him take a step backward into the passage, and at once had the unkind thought that he wished to hide his face from me in the dimmer light. But was it really an unkind thought, or was it a natural suspicion after seeing the look of diabolical hatred of which I knew his face to be capable?

"You must rest now," he said again. "My only concern is for your well-being and happiness. I want you to be happy here at Candlewyck, my dear. But I must caution you, even though I think you have learned this for yourself, never again to go near the edge of the cliff. It is a dangerous place. The edge itself sometimes crumbles; there are stones to trip the unwary foot; grass is slippery. Remember, stay away from the cliff."

I struggled to collect my thoughts and appear calm. "Should there not be a fence?" I succeeded in saying.

"Rest, my dear," Mr. Paget-Poole told me yet again. "I will bring you something to soothe your nerves."

And, saying only that, he withdrew from the doorway and I heard his step retreating down the passage.

What was I to do? I was dizzy, not only with the fright I'd had, but with the myriad of ideas swirling through my head. Candlewyck, a beautiful and wonderful home, now appeared to be as threatening as the door to Hell itself. Crickback, a monster, had turned into my savior. Mr. Paget-Poole, the gentleman of my dreams, suddenly had the look of a fiend. And next door, in the very next room, only inches away at the other side of the wall, another creature like myself lived a life of imprisonment and dread, I was certain of it now. I had seen her, and the look of fear upon her face. I had heard her the night before. It had been no dream. Oh, what was I to do?

I was so lost in these frightening reveries that I was startled when Mr. Paget-Poole appeared once again in the doorway.

"Here you are, my dear," he said, and extended toward me a crystal goblet containing a cloudy liquid. "Drink this and it will ease your nerves. When you have had a rest, and only then, please join me in the music room."

I crossed the room quickly and took the goblet from him.

This time, smiling still, he closed the door behind him as he turned away.

I dared not drink the potion he had brought me, for I was certain it was a cup of the most lethal sort of *poison!* Without a further thought, I carried it into the bedroom, went to the open window, leaned out, and poured the liquid from the glass. I heard it splash on the ground below.

Then I threw myself across the bed and gave myself up to weeping.

All was lost. I was no doubt a prisoner here, like the tortured inmate of the adjoining room, and all my pretty dreams of the future had turned to dust!

Chapter XI

Somehow, I dozed.

And as I dozed, I had a dream.

I dreamt that I had lived for some while at Candlewyck. It was a lovely and a happy place, filled with warmth and light and laughter. The roses grew high against the house and the chill of outdoors never came within.

The house was filled with servants, all happy in their work. Crickback was one of their number, and although he retained his incongruous name, he was a tall and handsome fellow whose greatest pleasure in life was derived from attending on me.

But no servant could ever attend as faithfully as did my own beloved husband, the master of Candlewyck, Mr. Paget-Poole himself, none other. For, yes, he had come, in time, to love me as I had loved him from our first moment of meeting, and our wedded life was bliss.

His young sister lived with us at Candlewyck and was my great boon companion. We tended to the gardens together, sang songs together at the pianoforte, sewed together, and took long walks along the cliff together, staring out to sea, and had nothing but the grandest times. And every morning she crept into my chambers and called my name softly until I awoke . . .

"Amanda."

I stirred.

"Amanda."

I stirred again, but clung still to my dream.

"Amanda, are you there?"

Alas, dreams tell us only how we would wish things to be. My eyes opened even as my thoughts yearned backward to my imagined happiness. But this was no dream. I sat up. The window was still open. My dress was still stained with grass and mud. My fingers still ached from clutching at the earth. And from the other side of the wall came the sobbing voice from the night before, my fellow prisoner, calling, "Amanda, Amanda, Amanda, are you there?"

Chapter XII

"I saw the whole thing," Mary Cantrell whispered to me through the wall. "Crickback is a good man, an angel of mercy who would save me if he could. But he is paralyzed with fear. He tried to save you. He saw you walking and standing near the edge of the cliff and at once ran to pull you away, or possibly he wished to warn you to run, run for your life! But even as he drew near, you slipped and nearly fell. If he had not already been hurrying toward you—oh, the thought is too terrible."

The sobs that formed her principal vocabulary threatened to overwhelm her again, but, with some effort, she forced them back.

"Amanda, you must listen to me," she said. "Listen to me carefully. Are you still there?"

"Yes," I whispered. I was frozen with fear at the things I imagined she was about to tell me.

"Listen," she said again. "You must get away from here. Get away at once. *Get away!* Never mind about me. I am locked in and nothing can save me now. But you still have your freedom, enough at least to permit you to escape. Oh, please do not waste another minute. Get away from Candlewyck and save yourself from the fate that awaits you!"

What could it be? I shuddered to think. Nothing I could conjure up from my wildest nightmares seemed the equal of what Mary Cantrell feared.

"I must think," I whispered in reply. "I must think and collect myself."

"Oh, hurry," cried Mary Cantrell.

I stood up and moved away from the wall. What was I to do? My heart was hammering wildly within me. Remembering Aunt Beatrice's advice, I took several very deep breaths to steady my nerves. I thought a bit of fresh air would help me think and stepped over to the window.

In contrast to everything else in the world, it seemed, the air outside was fresh and clear. I leaned on the sill of the window and bent forward to look out. As I did so, I happened to glance downward, and there below me was a dreadful sight.

I had earlier poured the cloudy liquid brought me by my employer out of that same window, and had heard it strike the rosebushes below. Now I looked down on those same rosebushes and saw that every one touched by the liquid was blackened and ruined, as if withered by the raging fires of Hell. But the drink had been intended for me, and the fate of the rosebushes had nearly been my own!

I had to press my fist against my mouth to keep myself from screaming.

Chapter XIII

"Mary!" I cried against the wall, once I had regained my composure.

"Amanda!" I heard her call in return.

"Mary, we must get out of here as quickly as possible."

"No," she said, "I am lost already. Save yourself!"

"I will not," I told her. I had made the decision without even thinking on it. How could I run away to save myself, and leave a fellow creature to suffer the very fate that I myself had fled? No, the thought was unsupportable. I could not do it.

"We will flee together," I whispered hurriedly. "But first you must tell me your condition. Then we can formulate a plan to effect our escape. Hurry now! Tell me what has happened to you."

There was some further exchange of this sort between us, but after a little while I was able to convince Mary Cantrell, who would willingly have suffered her fate alone, that I would not leave Candlewyck without her. At last she consented to tell me her tale, and from the very first shuddering words she spoke, it made my flesh crawl to hear it.

"I was alone in the world," she began, "with only a maiden aunt, whom I loved dearly, to think about me. My aunt was aging, however, and suffering from ever longer spells of weakness, and we both realized that her end was coming near.

" 'Find a position for yourself,' she told me repeatedly. 'You must prepare a place for yourself in the world, for I have nothing but your memories of me to leave you when I am gone.' It broke my heart to hear such words, but I had to admit the truth of them.

"My aunt's health was failing every day, and then one morning she was no more. Overcome with grief as I was, I felt with equal force the fact that I was now utterly alone in the world and thrown entirely on my own meager resources. I was qualified to do a little sewing, perhaps to give instruction on the pianoforte, and to be a congenial companion to a lady. I have been told more than once that

I possess a pleasant voice and that I read aloud well. Those were my few talents.

"As for money, I had only the few coins that had been in Auntie's purse and the few pounds she had kept tucked up in her mattress, enough to last a month or two if I was frugal.

"I had to do something, and quickly.

"My plan—I have always been adept at planning on my own; it is only the resources that I have lacked—was to write a letter in answer to every advertisement I could find in the newspapers from persons requiring the services of a tutor or governess or companion. In each letter, I stated my qualifications honestly. I was, as you can guess, turned down by every one, with the single exception of Mr. Paget-Poole of Candlewyck."

"So you are not related to him!" I cried out. I had not wished to interrupt her recital, but I could not contain my relief at this news.

"Oh, no!" Mary cried. "Heaven forbid that any God-fearing person should be related to such a *monster of depravity!*"

"Depravity!" I gasped. I could not prevent myself from crying out the word.

"Oh, dear Amanda," Mary said gently. "My heart goes out to you, for you have not yet learned the worst of what I have to tell you."

"Go on," I breathed.

With trembling voice, Mary Cantrell resumed her story. "I came here with the expectation of being companion to the lady of the house. I was a little surprised that there was no lady in evidence, and no servants, only Crickback to keep the entire establishment, but Mr. Paget-Poole was charming and reassuring and told me repeatedly that there was all the time in the world for that. Three days passed in this manner and I became more and more alarmed. None of my enquiries received straightforward answers.

"And there was something further that I shudder now to recount, just as I shuddered at the time.

"He looked at me in a way that no one had ever gazed upon me before. There was a kind of fire in his eyes, something I can only describe as a sort of *lurid hunger*. His gaze lingered on me at such length sometimes that I felt my flesh crawl beneath my clothing. He seemed to be studying me, measuring me in some secret way, and at the same time I thought he was watching some private scene transpiring in his thoughts, although I could not imagine what the nature of it might be."

"Oh!" I cried.

"He looked at me and looked at me, all the while rubbing his hands together in the most hideous fashion, until I couldn't stand it any longer. And so I confronted him with it. I demanded to know why he looked at me thus. And I demanded further that he introduce me at once to the lady of the house so that I might take up my proper duties. And my courage in thus confronting him is what brought about my downfall.

"No sooner had I spoken than he rushed across the room and took a painfully tight grip on my upper arm. I thought he was going to strike me with his other hand, and he raised his arm to do so, but then had a change of mind. It was then, dear Amanda, that I learned what my fate was to be.

" 'No, my child,' he said to me, leering in the most terrifying and lascivious—yes, that is the word—the most lascivious way. 'We don't want your beauty spoiled, do we?' he said. 'Oh, no, you must be pure and perfect so that gentleman callers will beat a path to your door.' Those were his very words and I shall never—no, never!—forget them."

I could barely breathe, so great was the wave of horror that washed over me. And this was to be my fate too. I hardly understood it, but I knew it was altogether too terrible to contemplate.

"I struggled," Mary Cantrell continued, "but of course he was too strong for me. He dragged me roughly up the stairs and pushed me to the floor in this room. For what seemed like hours, he stood above me and described, in words I hardly understood, exactly what would befall me."

"What?" I whispered.

"No," Mary said, "it is better that such thoughts are forever foreign to you. Suffice it to say that I thought I recognized a few of the words he used and could piece out some of the others. That is as much as you need to know. The only other thing is that he meant to lure other young women here, of whom you are the second, and install them—imprison them!—in the house. And then he meant to . . . Oh, it is too terrible!"

"What?" I cried. "What?"

"He meant to bring . . . men . . . here . . . and to . . . to set a . . . a fee . . . *for their pleasure!*"

At that, I could bear no more. I swooned.

Chapter XIV

When I recovered, I was lying on the floor and Mary Cantrell was calling my name anxiously through the wall.

I shook my head to clear it, and then the enormity of our situation rushed in on me with full force. We had to do something. We had to get away from Candlewyck. And since I alone was as yet unrestrained, our salvation depended on me.

"I'm all right now," I told Mary. "Yes, I am quite in control of myself. It was only the shock that took me for a moment."

I was not well at all, in truth, but swooning was not going to help matters. I am not by nature a brave person, but Mary Cantrell's courage in reciting her tale so straightforwardly conveyed to me a little of her own strength.

I had only one overpowering thought. *We must devise our escape, and that at once!*

My thoughts raced ahead with schemes and possibilities.

"First, we must join forces," I told her. I found I was short of breath with worry and excitement and the proximity of danger. My words came in a tumble. "There is only a wall to separate us. We must break through it!"

Mary Cantrell at once fell in with my scheme.

Each of us, on our own separate sides of the wall, ran our fingertips over the surface and examined it minutely. As I did so, I was struck by the size of the wardrobe that stood against the middle of the wall. At once I called to Mary. Did she perhaps have a wardrobe that was placed with its back to this same wall? She did! Hope sprang up in my bosom. The first step in my plan was falling into place. We would, by whatever means were at our disposal, break through the wall behind the wardrobe and use the wardrobe itself to conceal our efforts and our progress.

Mary approved the plan. But how, she asked, will we ever move the wardrobes? I studied my own. It matched me in height and was the width of my own spread arms. I leaned against it. It would not move. In her room, Mary examined her own and reached the same conclusion. Even before we could translate it into action, our plan seemed doomed to failure!

"Wait!" Mary cried. Crickback, she said, could move the wardrobe easily if he could be gotten to my room on some pretext that would not arouse the master's suspicion.

Crickback! Of course! Had he not saved my life, thereby risking the wrath of his master? If he had done that, perhaps he would do this as well. I told Mary I would find some excuse to bring him to my room.

But how was I to accomplish this? Mr. Paget-Poole himself had come to my room personally each time I had required attention. I racked my brain seeking a solution, and then I hit on one. I would say that, in my distress following the day's events, I had dropped a button while repairing my dress and it had rolled out of reach beneath the wardrobe.

I took several deep breaths to steady my nerves before venturing from the room. Then, setting my face into an expression of what I imagined to be feminine anxiety, rather than the determination I truly felt, I strode purposefully across the bedroom and the sitting room, before I might lose my nerve, and reached for the handle of the door.

The door would not open. It was firmly locked, and would in no way yield to my efforts. Now I too was forever *imprisoned* at Candlewyck!

Chapter XV

The mind, we have learned in this present Age of Wonders, is a marvelous instrument, although few people, I think, ever use its powers to their fullest extent. It is only in time of crisis, when we are in mortal danger or facing impending ruin, that we poor humans find the means of unlocking that great reservoir of courage and invention which we always have at our disposal but which usually remains barred to us.

It was so with me when I found the door of my room locked against me.

Without crying out or otherwise notifying Mary Cantrell of this new and unsettling—indeed, this apparently devastating—development, I retreated to one of the armchairs in the sitting room to think things through as best I could. I myself was surprised at my own state of calm. I compelled myself, by sheer force of will, to remain so. I *would not* yield to fright.

I put several questions to myself. Was our situation, in fact, hopeless? True, it appeared so, but was it not also true that I could see freedom merely by glancing out the window? The grass was still green, the sun still shone brightly, the waves still crashed against the rocks, birds still sang with all their usual merriness. Freedom was not a distant country, it was ready to hand. No, our situation was not without hope.

Secondly, I asked myself if we were merely two females alone in the world. And again the answer was no, for did we not have Crickback, here within the house, as an ally? Of course we did.

And thirdly, I asked myself if we were surrounded by a raging army of enemies. And the answer was that we were not. There was but one, Mr. Paget-Poole himself.

After putting these questions to myself, and answering them thus, I had to conclude that our situation was, in point of fact, not so hopeless as it appeared. All that was required was a workable plan to effect our escape.

But what was that plan to be?

I knew that poor Mary Cantrell eagerly awaited my return with news of bringing Crickback to move the wardrobe. Innocent thing, unaware of the true extent of our plight! But I had already made up my mind that I would not address her again until I had devised a suitable means of winning our freedom. Much of my own new-found strength, I knew, derived from her courage and stoical patience, and I meant to repay her for that by sparing her the news of the locked door until I had a means of overcoming it.

But what was to be my plan?

I had to fight hard against despair, for, try as I might, I could think of nothing, nothing at all. And all the while I struggled, time was racing past and narrowing our chances with every tick of the clock.

And then I hit upon a daring scheme that I recognized at once as the product of sheer desperation. It might work, I saw that in the instant it occurred to me, but it might win us our freedom only *at the cost of our lives!*

Chapter XVI

Mary Cantrell gasped a little, as I had done myself, when I told her of my plan, but she agreed that it was our only chance. Now it was simply a matter of waiting for the opportune moment.

I say "simply," but it was not a simple matter at all. Terrible worries assailed me, and fears all the more intense because it was possible now actually to glimpse freedom. So many things could go wrong, so many crucial moments that might turn suddenly to our disadvantage.

The waiting was all the more painful, too, because Mary and I must await the working out of destiny alone, in our separate cells. Oh, how I longed to gaze upon the face of my sister in suffering, to hold her hand, to clasp her to my bosom as I longed for her to clasp me. Strangers to each other in so many ways, yet we were as one in our anxiety and in our determination to escape the fate that threatened us.

Many an hour through the course of that long day did we spend crouching by the wall, whispering to each other. She told me of her dear departed aunt who had treated her so kindly, and I told her of my beloved Aunt Beatrice. The telling made me sad because I knew the dear old lady was in danger, if we did not succeed in escaping from Candlewyck, of receiving the dreadful news of either my disappearance or my death.

Yes, death! For Mary and I had made a solemn pact together, whispered in shaking voices through the wall, that if our plan of escape failed but did not bring about our deaths, we would each of us, murmuring a hasty prayer, fling ourselves from our windows to the stony terrace below. Even if that was the cost of escaping, the wicked man who now imprisoned us would never, we had sworn, wreak upon us the fate *even worse than death* that he had planned to be our lot.

Outside the windows, the day, like our hopes, grew dark and began to fade.

Would we never be sent any food? Were we to be left to starve to death in isolation? No, not even our jailer could be that cruel. And would that not, besides, thwart his own wicked plans for us? He had to send us food sooner or later.

We waited, and whispered, and prayed, and watched, at the windows, the day grow darker still.

And then there was a knocking at my door. I leapt up, stifling a cry. Even through the wall, I could hear Mary's sharp intake of breath.

At last the fateful moment had arrived. Now I would be tested to the utmost.

I rose, took a deep breath, composed myself—I could actually feel my back stiffen with resolve—and walked slowly toward the door. I was ready. I knew what I had to do. And I prayed that God would forgive me.

Chapter XVII

I called out, "Yes?" and was answered by a wordless grunt, a sound that yet expressed a world of kindness.

It was Crickback, as we had prayed it would be.

Mr. Paget-Poole had shown me to the room and had brought me the terrible drink himself, but I had not thought his "courtesy" would extend to carrying meals up the stairs, and indeed it did not.

Crickback, I quickly deduced, had been given the key to my room —perhaps the same key would even work in Mary's door!—and had unlocked the door already. But his innate good manners—oh, how my judgment of the fellow had been revised!—had compelled him to knock politely upon the door rather than merely throwing it open at his will.

I put my hand upon the doorknob. Yes, it turned at my touch. I pulled the door open.

Crickback was alone. That was one of the two principal items of information I was seeking, and I was not disappointed. All might have been lost had there been someone with him. And the other things I sought? Had he brought them? Yes, yes, there they were upon the tray!

"Come in, Crickback," I said quickly.

He made a lengthy sound which I interpreted to mean, "I've brought you something to eat."

I directed him to place the tray on the table between the two armchairs, but in truth it was not the food he'd brought that interested me. No, not that. He'd brought the very tools for the first step in our plan, and with them something else that I meant to be the true key that would unlock Candlewyck for Mary Cantrell and myself.

He had brought a candle, as we had prayed so fervently, and its little yellow flame seemed to flicker madly as if in rhythm with the beating of my heart. That flame meant life, and freedom, and escape from the clutches of the monster.

"Here," I said, and watched Crickback as he set the tray upon the table. I could tell from his circumspect and agitated manner that he wished to deliver himself, if he could, of some heartfelt sentiment, but I knew too that he was prevented from doing so by what could only be termed abject fear. My heart went out to him, as it would to any fellow sufferer, for was not the poor hunchback as much a prisoner as Mary and myself?

He took some little time settling the tray and its contents to his satisfaction, and I knew that this was only a means of delaying his departure.

"Crickback," I said, using a voice that I hoped would compel him to meet my gaze directly. He twisted around at his name and looked at me. "Crickback, will you be bringing a tray to Mary Cantrell as well?"

He grunted, all the time watching my face, although I could see the fear that clouded his eyes.

"I do not feel very well, Crickback," I told him, "and I expect I shall be eating slowly. I think it will be some time before I am ready to have the tray cleared away." I spoke very deliberately and looked at him in a very meaningful manner, trying to convey silently the message I dared not speak aloud.

He grunted again. He understood!

"And one other thing before you go, Crickback."

At once he looked fearful. Could this be the end of our plan?

"I have carelessly dropped a button," I said, "which I need to repair my dress, and it has rolled beyond my reach. In the bedroom," I added casually, "beneath the wardrobe. Do you think you could move the wardrobe for me?" I said all this and then held my breath.

Crickback hesitated. What thoughts and emotions, I wondered desperately, were racing through his mind? What thoughts, indeed, were racing through my own? Did I want him to know our plan so that he might the better aid us and, in the process, be sure of saving himself? Or was it better that he not know, thus safeguarding our secret? I myself did not know the answer.

And then the tension was broken and Crickback twisted around without a word and moved sideways toward the bedroom. I closed my eyes for an instant and murmured a silent prayer for his salvation.

With seemingly no effort at all, he gripped the end of the wardrobe and swung it away from the wall. Never once did he search the floor for a button, so I was certain he had fallen in willingly with my ruse. This emboldened me. I determined to give him a clue to the rest of our plan that would prepare him for a suitable course of action later on.

As I led the way back to the sitting room, I said, "And I shall be very careful with the candle. These old houses are very susceptible to fire."

Insofar as such a sadly deformed creature's head may be said to snap at all, his head snapped around and his eyes met mine. A light of brilliant intelligence burned there, and something else too, something I can only call compassion. Yes, he understood, and he would help us if he could. All that was spoken by his eyes.

And a moment later, he was gone. I heard the key turn in the lock, but I had expected that. In fact, I would not have wanted him to do otherwise. His master might take a notion to try the door himself, and it was essential that he find it stoutly locked as he had ordered.

No sooner was the key withdrawn from the lock than I hurried around the room, lighting the few candles with which it was provided. Then I raced back to the bedroom, knelt behind the wardrobe, and pressed my ear against the wall. I heard, faintly, Crickback's knock, the door being opened, the rattle of silverware as a tray was set down, and the door being closed once again. And finally, I heard Mary Cantrell's whisper, telling me that we were once again alone.

I wasted not a second. Breathless, I rushed back to the sitting room and snatched what I needed from the tray. I knew that in her room, Mary was doing the same.

Crouching on the floor by the wall, and with only a few hastily whispered words of encouragement, we set to work.

Suddenly the task—and therefore our entire plan of escape!—seemed utterly impossible. We would never break through the wall *using only a knife and fork!*

Chapter XVIII

After that moment of doubt, I screwed up my courage and went at it with a will. On the other side of the wall, I could hear Mary doing the same.

It was terrible, hopeless, dispiriting work, but we persevered. Plunge in the knife, twist as far as strength permitted, gouge and tear at the wall, then apply the little fork to enlarge the space by a fraction of an inch. Then begin the cycle all over again. Plunge, twist, gouge, tear, then use the fork again. But we kept at it, resting frequently, for it was hot and heavy work.

I hardly knew how much time had passed but then, suddenly, we broke through the wall. The barrier had been breached!

The plan was working, and we went at it again with renewed vigor.

Soon, within minutes, I should see my sister in suffering and fold her in my arms!

The wall crumbled away beneath our frenzied attack, the hole growing larger and larger. Now, with success so near, we dared not speak until the hole had been enlarged enough to permit Mary to pass through. Oh, would it never be finished! We plunged, gouged, tore, bending both knife and fork, but at last the task was done.

And when finally Mary had passed through the wall and we stood before each other, neither of us could speak, so overcome were we with emotion.

We held each other's hands, studied each other's faces, fell into each other's arms, like prisoners suddenly released from a dozen years in the foul clutches of Hottentots.

When, fighting back the tears of joy and relief, we at last stood apart from each other, I had an opportunity to study the face I had until then only imagined.

Mary Cantrell was lovely, exquisite. Slight, as a woman should be, she yet somehow commanded attention. Her skin was pale and fair, the product of nature as much as the sad result of her imprisonment, and showed off her dark hair to advantage, but her most striking feature was, without a doubt, her eyes. They were dark and deep, filled, I thought at once, with a wisdom beyond her years, and warm and loving at the same time. She was dressed prettily but plainly and she wore no jewelry or decoration of any sort. Mary Cantrell needed no adornment. She had those eyes!

But we could no longer give vent to our emotion. We had to press forward with the next step in our plan.

Together, each of us emboldened by our success so far, we rushed into the sitting room. Three candles flickered fitfully, making eerie shadows dance about the walls, shadows, I thought, of demons who laughed and capered and mocked at our hopes. I pressed my lips together and resolved to ignore them. Soon there would be worse than those shadows to contend with in the room.

Now for the next step in the plan.

"The bedroom," I whispered to Mary. She nodded.

We each took a candle and, carefully shielding the flame, walked slowly to the bedroom.

"The bed," I whispered, and again saw Mary nod.

We moved to opposite sides of the bed. It was then, just before the most decisive moment in our scheme, and the most dangerous, that my courage nearly failed me.

"We must, Amanda, we must," Mary said softly. "It is the only way."

We had worked it out together, step by step, weighing every move.

We would set fire to the bed. It would burst into flames and smoke. We would retreat at once to the sitting room, crying as loudly as we could for help. Of necessity, Crickback and Mr. Paget-Poole would come running to our aid. They must. Crickback would come of his own volition—and I had given him a clue to our plan, besides—and the master must needs come to save his home, to save Candlewyck. They would rush in at the sitting room door and, in the confusion, Mary and I would slip out and effect our escape.

"God be with us," I murmured.

"God be with us," Mary echoed.

We bent together and touched the flames to the edge of the counterpane.

The flames caught, fed on themselves, and rushed hungrily upward. Thick gray smoke billowed from the bed. In a moment the foot of the bed was engulfed in flames.

We rushed back to the sitting room and began calling out through the door.

"Help! Help! Oh, please help! Fire! Fire! We shall be burned alive! Help! Help!"

We stopped a moment to lean against the door and draw breath again, for our hearts were pounding so hard that we could barely speak.

"Help!" I cried again, and was suddenly choked by a violent fit of coughing. The excitement and danger had taken my breath away.

Though racked with coughing and blinded by tears, I saw that Mary Cantrell was in the same state.

And then, with a sensation of horror I could not previously have imagined to be possible, I realized what was happening to us. We were being choked by the smoke from the very fire we had set!

Of course we had anticipated smoke. Indeed, the smell of it was meant to draw our rescuers. Now it was billowing in great dark clouds out of the bedroom and threatening to engulf the sitting room. And there was not a sound of racing footsteps on the stairs or in the passage. Something had happened to Crickback, and the master of Candlewyck meant to leave us to our fate. Within minutes, perhaps within mere seconds, we would die of *suffocation!*

Chapter XIX

We dropped to the floor where the air was a little clearer, and used nearly the last of our breath to cry, "Help! Help!" until our voices failed us.

And then we heard footsteps pounding in the passage. Poor Crickback—what had become of him?—could not move that way. It must be Mr. Paget-Poole, coming to save us.

But this was not to be. It was indeed he who came to a halt outside the door, but our salvation was not his goal.

"So you thought to fool me!" he cried in a voice that shook with rage. "You thought to make a fool of *me!* Well, you shall not succeed, my dears! Set a fire, will you? Well, then, you shall meet your deaths in it! Choke, ha ha, suffocate, yes, and while death comes near, think how foolish you have been. You might have lived in luxury and comfort, but no, you chose death. Well, then, let it be! Let the flames consume you! Ha ha ha!"

The fire was crackling loudly now in the next room, but the monster's hideous laughter rang in our ears. *We were lost, lost, lost!*

But there is a flame that burns in the human heart even more brightly than the flames that now threatened to consume us: the flame of life itself, the yearning of the human spirit to preserve its existence, even if in pain and even if for only a few seconds more. I saw that flame burning in Mary Cantrell's eyes, and I felt its heat in my own bosom.

"The window!" I cried. "Air!"

Keeping close to the floor—what a spectacle we would have been, had anyone been watching—we crept across the room and raised our heads at the sill of one of the windows. Gratefully we drew great draughts of cool evening air into our parched lungs. Our lives would be preserved for a few precious seconds longer.

We clasped each other for comfort but great choking sobs made any speech impossible. This was truly the end. We were done for.

In the passage outside the door, Mr. Paget-Poole, the cruelest beast that ever walked the face of the earth in human disguise, continued to rage, his words now incomprehensible above the roaring of the fire. Flames now licked at the doorway between the bedroom and sitting room. In a moment, our suffering would be ended.

We turned our eyes away to look out the window at the freedom we had nearly reached. Our fingers knotted tightly together, for each of us knew what we must do now. We had pledged it. We would neither live as the monster's prisoners nor die at his will.

We rose a little from the floor and leaned across the sill. It was a lovely night, with a clear sky and brilliant moon turning the dark world silver with its light. There would be no more such nights or such moons for us. Together, we looked down. The moonlight fell full upon the stone terrace below. That was where we would end.

I shuddered at the thought and, in the same instant, felt the *Angel of Death* touch the back of my neck with fingers as cold as the grave!

Chapter XX

But it was not the Angel of Death. It was an *Angel of Mercy*. It was Crickback!

"Crickback! Oh, Crickback!" I cried. I could not help myself. Instantly, I feared that Mr. Paget-Poole had heard me. But, no, he could not have done, for behind us the flames were roaring ever louder.

But what was Crickback doing here, above us but upside-down, and suspended miraculously in midair? The poor man was outside the window, hands scrabbling at the rough wall of the house. He was, so it appeared, in such a desperate plight that his speech was no more comprehensible than that of a beast in the wild.

A sudden jerk of his limbs sent Crickback swinging away to one side of the window. I saw his lips writhing in an agonizing attempt to speak. In frustration, he pointed one finger upward. There was no explanation.

He had somehow fixed a stout rope to a parapet on the roof and thus lowered himself down to the level of our window. Now it was all clear to me, and I saw the rest of the rope swinging free below his dangling form, stretching all the way to the terrace far below. The moonlight struck the rope, turning it into a silver thread, and casting its writhing shadow against the stone wall of the house.

But how were we to be saved? Did he mean to carry us? How then would he cling to the rope himself? Surely the three of us would plummet together to our deaths.

Crickback had one hand free and was desperately struggling to catch the top of the window frame to steady himself. With Mary grasping me round the waist for security, I stretched to my limit and was just able to clutch at the man's collar. I pulled, and he swung a little closer.

Somehow, by means I could not possibly describe, the poor deformed creature was able—perhaps even aided in this by the compactness of his form—to swing himself about until he was seated on the edge of the windowsill. His body was positively shaking with his exertions. Poor twisted thing, perched there on a window ledge, high above the ground! He had risked his life in an effort to save ours! Even if we all three perished now, I knew that I should die content in the knowledge that there was such courage and charity and self-sacrifice in another human being!

The smoke now nearly filled the sitting room. Flames, like the tongue of a ravening beast licked farther and farther out of the bedroom. Mary and I clutched our skirts about us. Over the roar of the fire, we could just make out the crazed screams of Mr. Paget-Poole. Surely all reason had deserted him. The evil ways in which he had lived his life, and the depravity of his plan for us, combined now with finding himself foiled in his foul scheme, had thoroughly unhinged him.

Crickback plucked at our arms. He was jabbering frantically but there was no possibility of deciphering his meaning. What did he want us to do? Straining his already twisted body into an even more contorted pose, he managed to slap himself repeatedly about the neck and shoulders. Could that be it? Yes, I saw it now. We were to throw our arms about his neck and cling there tightly, and he would lower all three of us down on the rope.

It was a desperate plan, but it was the only plan that remained to us. Sobbing our gratitude to him, and prayers of entreaty to our Maker, we flung our arms about him and clung on for dear life itself.

Slowly, slowly, Crickback settled his grip on the rope above his head, and then pushed himself away from the ledge and the wall of the house. Mary and I were dragged across the sill and out at the window. I expected at every second to be dashed to the stones of the terrace, but no, we swung there, *suspended helplessly* between heaven and earth!

Chapter XXI

It seemed an eternity, but, with scrupulous caution, Crickback began slowly lowering our combined weight by carefully moving one hand and then the other down the taut length of the rope. We swung this way. We swung that way. Many times we were smashed against the rough wall of the house. Our clothing must have been in a terrible state, and our elbows and shoulders suffered bruises that must perforce stay with us a long time. But poor Crickback suffered worst of all. He supported the whole weight of two terrified females who must, the whole while, have been nearly choking him to death. But even while we held our breath and prayed, the wall beside us appeared to creep upward inch by painful inch. And then, at last, several seconds ahead of poor Crickback, Mary's feet and mine touched the solid ground of the terrace.

We were down! We were saved! We were free!

We could barely stand upright, so weak were our knees, but we were filled with joy and with gratitude to our savior. Oh, how sweet was the air of freedom, so long tasted but so little appreciated before!

Then Crickback too had reached the earth. He stood a moment, wheezing, drawing air into his lungs. Then he began jabbering madly again and drawing us away from the house.

"Run!" he cried, and we had no trouble understanding his meaning.

We ran, the three of us, with little Crickback leading the way—for Mary and I were shaking so much that we could barely move—across the sloping lawn and away from the house. We ran to the right, toward where the driveway approached from the road, in danger at every step of slipping on the dewy grass, but with our path illuminated by the whitely glowing orb of the moon. Crickback reached the safety of the woods before us and stopped there to wait, frantically gesturing at us to hurry.

At the edge of the woods, we stopped and looked back whence we had come. It was the last sight we should ever have of Candlewyck. The great house, with its parapets and towers, was in darkness, except for the firelight illuminating that single room on the topmost floor, the room that had nearly been my lifelong prison, and worse.

What a picture we must have presented! Two terrified young women, clad only in our simple dresses, running down the moonlit slope, with the great hulking house behind us, and firelight shining from that window. The image haunts me still.

But we were free, that was the main thing now, and it filled us with joy. Free, Mary and myself, and in the process, poor Crickback had won his own liberty from the cruelest of masters.

But our joy was premature, for *another terrible shock* awaited us still.

Chapter XXII

Crickback clutched at our hands and cried, "Run! Run away!" His words rang out clearly in the night, so great was his passion to see us saved. "Run! Run!"

"Yes, come!" I said, and Mary and I turned to run down the driveway through the wood.

We had taken only a few steps before we realized that Crickback was not running with us.

"Crickback!" Mary Cantrell and I cried out as one.

The little man was a dark shadow against the moonlit lawn. We saw him cock his head on one side, in a gesture expressive of the most profound emotion.

And it was no doubt that same emotion that made the words he spoke then issue with perfect clarity from his lips.

"No," he said. "You must run and save yourselves. But I cannot go away. Mr. Paget-Poole has been my master all my life and, in his way, has provided me a home and useful employment, without which I should have been a beggar on the highway, or worse, and the butt of little boys' teasings and pointing fingers. No, I cannot run away now. I must go back and try to save him. I must! Please understand. Run now, as fast as you can, and save yourselves!"

And with that, Crickback turned and began running, in his curious sidewise fashion but at great speed, back up the lawn toward the house.

There was nothing we could do to stop him, and in a moment we saw him disappear through the front door into the darkness of the house. The same poor creature who had just risked his life to save us would now risk it again to save his wicked master. Mary and I held each other tightly but neither of us breathed a word in the face of such devotion.

We stood there, immobilized by terror and the events of this night, for some minutes. The flames that had been licking round the window frames on the top floor had now, it seemed, moved on to other rooms. And suddenly, as a strong breeze rushed in from the sea, the whole top floor of the house was alight. We were at some distance from it but, even so, we could hear the fury of the fire.

And Crickback had rushed back into that inferno!

It was cold comfort indeed, but within minutes we knew his sufferings could not have been long. The top floor blazed brightly, flames leaping from the windows, and then, with a deafening cacophony of splitting beams and rending walls, the top floor fell in and Candlewyck, that once grand house, collapsed inward upon itself. Within minutes only the stony shell remained, a blackened husk in the moonlight, the flames—like the very flames of Hell itself—having devoured all within.

Chapter XXIII

With some little difficulty, Mary and I found our way to the nearest village and threw ourselves upon the mercy of people who proved kinder in their hospitality than Mr. Paget-Poole. From there we were conveyed to the seaside village where Aunt Beatrice was visiting a friend. She devoted herself, for some weeks, to nursing us both back to health.

Mary stayed with us until her health was fully restored, but then, over the protests of both Aunt Beatrice and myself, she insisted that she must be on her way. We implored her to remain with us but, in her gentle way, she was adamant.

And then the appointed day came and she left us to make her way alone in the world. I have not laid eyes upon her since.

The ruins of Candlewyck yet stand upon the cliff, looking out toward the sea that still crashes below, but the spirit that once reigned there is long departed.

Mary Cantrell is gone too, although surely not in the same way. She left us with yet another expression of gratitude to me for saving her life. But if it is true that I did so, it is equally true that she saved mine, and that she gave me another gift besides. She taught me courage.

I do not know where she is now. Even so, I cannot help but think that, no matter what direction Mary Cantrell may take, she will touch the lives of those around her in the same way she touched mine.

The Queen of Kilimanjaro

"Harrumph!" said Colonel Sir Maurice Heywood Witherspoon again.

It must have been the third time he'd done it in what could not have been more than ten minutes. His voice was the only sound in the Reading Room. We members of the Adventurers Club are a quiet lot within those hallowed and restorative precincts, which, it must be remembered, are our retreat from the strenuous labors that earn us our continuance as members. Noise we have aplenty in our travels—think, for example, of the infernal chanting of the Hottentots in the night, and the hellish booming of their drums, the devils!—so it is frowned upon severely within the chambers of the Club. An effort had been raised, I knew, some while previously, among a number of the younger members, to find a way of silencing Witherspoon's harrumphing, but of course it came to nothing in the end. Witherspoon was regarded by many as the Club's bravest member. He had survived shipwreck in the Indian Ocean, poison darts from natives of both the Amazon and the Niger, imprisonment in the jungles of Ceylon, and an enforced marriage to a third cousin of Shaka-Zulu in a ceremony that customarily ended with the groom being eaten alive by the wife's family if his performance on the marriage night was not up to snuff. That was in Witherspoon's younger days, of course, but he had seen the lot and survived it all, a model for every one of us and an ornament to the English nation. There could be no question of speaking to him about his harrumphing.

Even so, three outraged harrumphs within ten minutes seemed extraordinary, and could only denote some terrible disturbance. I glanced over toward Witherspoon's chair across the top of my newspaper, and saw Carstairs and Reville doing the same across theirs. Witherspoon was perusing a letter, and a dark frown creased his forehead.

At the moment we three looked up, the old warrior raised his head from the page and exclaimed, "Gad!"

The three of us were on our feet at once, all thoughts of silence put aside.

Witherspoon had, over the years, so refined his vocabulary and patterns of speech, to coincide with his mature and advanced view of the world, that his vocal expressions now numbered only three. He said "Harrumph!" and he said "By Jove!" and either, depending on the subtlety of his inflection, could convey a vast range of meaning. But it was only in the most extraordinary and extreme of circumstances that he would permit himself to say "Gad!" I myself had heard him say it only twice before over the years, once in the Crimea and once at Rorke's Drift. Some members, Carstairs and Reville among them, had never heard him say it at all, so their shock may easily be imagined.

"Good God, man, what is it?" Carstairs cried.

Reville, always more reserved than Carstairs, said, "The letter. What news?"

I confined myself to, "Tell us, Witherspoon. Whatever it is, we are all in it together." It's a point I feel strongly on.

Witherspoon looked up and studied our faces while at the same time contemplating, as I thought, some dread vision that he saw only in his mind's eye. My thoughts raced, searching a mental catalogue of Club members who might be in grave dangers in the outermost reaches of the Empire or, worse still, beyond. But danger is our stock in trade here at the Club, so to speak, our meat and potatoes. No, something unimaginable was recounted in that letter. Nothing less could have made Witherspoon say, "Gad!"

"Tell us, Witherspoon," I said again.

In silence, his eyes darkened by tragedy, he handed me the letter.

I scanned it quickly while Carstairs and Reville waited, all impatience. When I was done, I could not contain my shock.

"Good God!" I exclaimed, "Berresford is dead!"

"Dead!" my listeners said together.

I raised a hand to silence them. "With permission," I said—I looked to Witherspoon, who nodded silently—"I will read the letter aloud."

The letter was addressed to Colonel Witherspoon in care of the Adventurers Club, Pall Mall, London. It was dated a little over a month previous. The paper itself was badly soiled and there was a rusty stain at one of the top corners. At some point in its travels the letter had been damaged and part of the message was missing, but there was enough there to give a brave man pause.

"My dear old friend," Berresford's letter began. "This is farewell, for by the time this letter reaches you, I shall be a dead man."

Reville drew in a sharp breath, and Carstairs went so far as to sit upon the arm of a chair.

"My expedition proceeded," the letter continued, "for some weeks exactly as planned. Identified six new kinds of gazelle, spotted some remarkable elands and kudu, and eleven species of bird previously uncatalogued. The shooting was remarkable, and we quickly gathered an impressive load of ivory and skins. Africa's wildlife is limitless; it will never run out. I had the good fortune to acquire the services of an intelligent and resourceful headman to keep the bearers in line. He is a Kikuyu named Jeremiah. Should you ever come this way, ask for him in Mombasa; they all know him there.

"But, no, old friend, you must not think of coming this way ever again, lest you suffer the fate that has befallen me. My strength is failing rapidly now and I must tell my tale briefly, not, to be sure, to make you grieve, but to keep the records of the Club complete.

"My expedition's proposed route is in the files of the Club, so it will be known to you. All was in order setting out from Mombasa and well into the highlands. Excellent shooting round about the Tsavo River, by the way. Excellent. We pressed on from there, but in a fortnight's time began experiencing some difficulty with the bearers. I truly believe I should not have got as far as I did had it not been for Jeremiah. Remarkable fellow in all respects, kept those beggars in line.

"Our goal of course was the mountain called by the natives hereabouts Kilimanjaro, which means 'head in the clouds' or 'whitehaired old man' or some such thing. At least, it means that in the language of one of the local tribes. In another language, though, it is said to mean 'burying place of strangers.' This, although I did not credit it when first I heard the translation, proved to be prophetic.

"Even with the bearers threatening to run off, however, we reached the jungle at the base of Kilimanjaro in due course. We pitched camp and I consulted with Jeremiah about the best route to the top. Much to my surprise, he advised me not to attempt it.

" 'But why not?' I asked him. 'You knew all along this was our goal.'

" 'I know that, Bwana,' he said, 'and I thought I had the courage to go with you. I thought so, Bwana; I would not lie to you, nor to any white chief from over the water. But now I tell you, I am afraid for myself, and I am afraid for you, for if you violate Kilimanjaro, you must do so without me. I will give you back the wages you have paid, Bwana, but I cannot go farther.'

"Well, you may imagine my consternation. To have him back out at this juncture! And he whom I had thought fearless, now professing himself afraid. I could not think what to make of it, and he was not much able to enlighten me. He seemed reluctant even to state his reasons, only muttered some nonsense about curses and native gods I had never heard tell of before this, and there was talk too of some fabulous treasure that belonged to the gods and of some fierce and savage tribe that guarded it at the top of the mountain. We talked late into the night, but I could not convince him that his fears were all mere superstition. This was all the more trying for me because I knew the fellow was no blackguard. If you can believe it, the man simply would not listen to reason.

"And then, in the morning, I found that every last one of the bearers had run off in the night, and taken most of the stores with them, the thieving rascals. Now there was only Jeremiah himself, and me. And one other person.

"My friend, I have a confession to make. I have not been completely open with you in the past. I have kept a secret.

"I have—had, I should say, for even as I write, I feel the effects of the poison spreading through my system—a ward, a girl of not more than a score of years, whom I have come to love and regard as I would a daughter of my own. How I came to be her guardian is of no moment now; I will say only that I first made her acquaintance in the port of Durban and that she might have perished there without the protection, instantly declared, of an Englishman. No civilized person would have done less.

"I have seen little enough of her, due to my extensive travels, but I know her to be a brave girl, nearly as brave, I think, as a man. In short, she begged permission to accompany me into the interior and, at length, weakened by her entreaties, I relented. I allowed her to come. And now I must face my end with the knowledge that I have very likely been the instrument of her death—or worse. And she so fine a young woman, in the full bloom of life, and—though she has never, to my knowledge, set foot in England—an Englishwoman besides!

"Her name . . ."

But here the letter was torn and its ghastly message interrupted. I turned it over to the second side, where it began in midsentence. I drew in a shuddering breath, and then began reading again.

". . . last we saw of Jeremiah. I should not be surprised if the poor fellow ended up in some tribal cookpot, for these bloody savages make no distinction between the meat of their own kind and that of white men.

"My strength fails me rapidly now. I must be brief, but there is little more to tell.

"After the loss of Jeremiah, the girl and I were taken within the hour, and the brutes accorded her no more respect than they offered me. When I protested in the name of God, England, and the Queen, the heathens thumped me across the head. I remember nothing after that until a band of Germans found me at the edge of a dirt track near the Tsavo River. I must have made my way down from the base of the mountain and then wandered in a delirium, for I had no recollection whatsoever of the time since I was struck. Indeed, I could barely speak at all, so weak had I become, and the Germans had little English, so anything I may have said to them is forever lost. They carried me as far as the rail line (the Kenya-Uganda Railway, you know, which is taking so blasted long to build) and thence I was conveyed to Mombasa where, shortly, I have no doubt, I shall breathe my last. The brutes of Kilimanjaro evidently introduced one of their foul poisons into my system, some substance that has partly destroyed my memory and is now rapidly consuming my body.

"But, dear friend, the foulest poison of all is the knowledge of my own guilt in endangering a sweet and innocent girl. She was alive the last time I saw her, but beyond that I cannot say.

"I am very weak now, and my eyes are failing me. Farewell, my friend, and be kind enough to express my final regards to my fellows of the Club."

The letter was signed, in a hand that had grown less steady with every line and was now barely decipherable, "George Taylor Berresford, M.A.C."

Silence enveloped us for some little while before anyone spoke. The someone was myself, although I could not keep the huskiness from my voice.

"I shall ask the chief steward to begin preparations at once for a brief memorial service and to arrange for Berresford's name to be inscribed on the brass plaque in the foyer."

Carstairs and Reville murmured their assent and Witherspoon, suffering the effects of grief as he was, said sadly, "Harrumph." The plan was approved.

"But, gentlemen," I said, "although poor Berresford, God rest his tormented soul, may be laid in the earth, we cannot do the same with the information we now possess. We cannot, on our honor as gentlemen and Members of the Adventurers Club. The matter is not finished. While a chance remains that the girl is still among the living, no effort must be spared in her behalf. We must go to Africa at once, find her, and fetch her out."

Witherspoon said, "By Jove!"

I looked at Carstairs and Reville, who agreed without hesitation.

"Well, then," I said. "I propose, gentlemen, that we devote the remainder of the day to settling our affairs in London. When I speak with the chief steward, I shall also ask him to arrange our passage."

"When shall we leave?" asked Reville, who was nothing if not practical and methodical.

"On the morrow," I told him.

"Tomorrow!" they said together.

"On the morrow, gentlemen," I said. "We assemble at the Club at eight and leave from here. Unless Colonel Witherspoon has an objection, I will assume the responsibilities of leadership at least until we are arrived at Mombasa. There, we can formulate such plans as are agreeable to us all."

"Harrumph, by Jove!" said Witherspoon, indicating his hearty approval.

We shook hands solemnly all round.

So it was agreed and we parted to see to our personal business without further delay.

Thus it was that I, Sir Clive Waterstone-Foyle, in the company of Colonel Sir Maurice Heywood Witherspoon, Charles Carstairs, and Lawrence Reville, Gentlemen both, and all Members of the Adventurers Club, of Pall Mall, London, set out for Africa once again, in June of 189–, vowing that, upon our arrival at Mombasa, we would first determine the location of Berresford's grave, pay our due respects there to a fellow Member, then organize an expedition up-country, follow his trail, such as we knew it from his abbreviated letter, locate the Germans, if possible, who had assisted him, locate Jeremiah, if he was still among the living, reach Kilimanjaro, climb it, find the girl, if God had spared her, free her from her heathen captors and fetch her out, or die in the attempt. It looked to be a matter of weeks, no more.

II
Plans Are Formulated at Sea

On the voyage out, I had time to contemplate the task that lay before us. We had, all four of us, faced worse, of course, much worse, but seldom had our goal seemed to lay such a personal burden on our shoulders. I myself could barely sleep at nights, for my thoughts were ravaged with memories of the brutal ceremonies and rituals I had seen practiced among the savages of the east African uplands. My own body is marked with two scars, among others, where a native assegai passed right through it on one occasion. I lost a finger to another tribe in a savage ceremony, but I don't like to talk about that. My companions had similar tales to tell.

Our thinking on the expedition ahead was not eased by our sea voyage. Choppy waters off the coast of France—the French do it deliberately somehow, I'll warrant—and choppier still in the Mediterranean. Blistering heat in the Red Sea—it will drive the inhabitants of both shores out of their minds one day, I have no doubt—and then hotter weather still in the Indian Ocean. All in a day's work, of course, as they say, but damned inconvenient. And the deck of the ship, naturally, was strewn the whole while with the lowest and laziest sort of evil-eyed Lascars, all eager to pick your pocket for tuppence if you once let down your guard.

I met Witherspoon one morning on the foredeck—the smell of the Lascars was less troublesome there with the ship making some speed at last as we neared the African coast—and we had a good and thoroughgoing conversation about our prospects once we put in at Mombasa.

"Harrumph," said Witherspoon, and fixed his gaze inquisitively upon me.

"Well, yes, I've given some thought to that," I said slowly. "I should think the Germans would turn up. Of course, there are great numbers of them in Tanganyika nowadays, farmers mostly—trying their damnedest to be Englishmen, if you ask me—but fewer in the region we'll be seeing. Hardworking fellows, for the most part, I think, and honest, once you get past that rough exterior. And naturally they all know one another, that lot always do. Find one German, find them all. No, we'll have no trouble on that score, mark my words."

Witherspoon thought it over and finally said, "Harrumph."

"I'm glad you agree," I said. "Then, of course, there's the matter of hearing whatever there is to hear about this Jeremiah fellow."

"By Jove!" said Witherspoon.

"Oh," I said, "I shouldn't think it would be as difficult as all that. No, no, I think not. Berresford's letter, remember, said that he was well known in Mombasa. We'll turn up someone who knew him before in Mombasa and may know something of his fate, I'm certain of that. We'll gather a great deal of information there. Yes, I'm sure we will. And, Witherspoon, if I may say so, my own African experience has been primarily in this region, in Kenya. I've had my time, of course, in southern Africa—Zululand, Matabeleland, all that ugly business in Natal and Bulawayo; you know it all yourself and never mind about Isandhlwana and Rorke's Drift—but it's eastern Africa I know best, Tanganyika, Kenya, Lake Victoria, Lake Rudolf, all that area round about there. Lovely country in parts, by the way, absolutely splendid. Flamingos at Lake Naivasha, you know, millions of 'em. Wasted on the natives, of course. Pity. Still, they'll thank us one day for bringing them Christianity and for civilizing them. Oh, yes, they will, I'm quite certain of it."

"Harrumph," Witherspoon murmured thoughtfully.

"The point is," I went on, "that I know these people well, and the area. Speak their lingo too, you know. Swahili, they call it. Oh, it's not much of a language, of course, but it seems to serve their purposes. I daresay that will stand us in good stead. And I have two dialects of the Kikuyu language and three of the Masai, besides."

Nodding, Witherspoon said, "Harrumph."

"So, in short, my feeling is that, if there is anything to be learned at Mombasa, we shall learn it. After that, it's merely a matter of getting up an expedition—headman, guide, bearers, provisions, what have you—and following the same trail as Berresford toward this mountain and then, if need be, up it to the top."

Witherspoon had been leaning on the rail, but now he stood straight again and turned to look me full in the face. "Harrumph," he said in the significant way he had.

"Yes, well," I replied slowly. "Yes, I do agree with you there. That is a serious point. The superstitions are all nonsense, of course, but it is equally true that the man who treats them lightly is a fool. Naturally, that wouldn't apply to Berresford. He no doubt had some good reason for pursuing his object, a reason his weakness did not allow him to commit to paper, poor fellow. But we shall find out just what the local superstitions are—knowing the lingo will come in handy there—and make our final plans accordingly. As I see it, it's just a matter of getting to Kilimanjaro, learning the lay of the land, winning the trust of the local tribes there, or, if they won't listen to reason, putting them down and then proceeding anyway."

Witherspoon lowered his head and fixed me with a look from beneath his shaggy white eyebrows. "Harrumph!" he said. "Harrumph!"

I did not reply at once, for the same thought had been troubling me.

"Yes," I said at last, "I quite agree. That is the single most bothersome question that needs answering. I would go so far as to formulate a rule on the subject. Whenever the natives babble of treasure, tread slowly. Indeed, I shall take care to include that maxim in my account of this undertaking. Many's the man who has ignored that rule to his cost. So, yes, I think you're right, Witherspoon, we shall have to seek out what tales of treasure we can hear. The final stages in our plan to rescue the girl may well depend on the nature of those very tales."

Witherspoon shook his head thoughtfully, then turned once again to the rail and a silent contemplation of the white crest that foamed across the bow of the ship. I joined him in the pastime. It is a common habit of travelers like ourselves to study the sea in this fashion, for another week may see us brought to our knees in the baking desert, or stranded in the jungle, or freezing on the side of a barren mountain. We were both lost in thought for some little while.

Then Carstairs and Reville joined us at the rail. Witherspoon greeted them with his customary "Harrumph," and then said, taking in all three of us in his glance, "Harrumph, harrumph."

I looked at Carstairs and Reville, and I am pleased to say that I saw agreement in their faces.

"I concur fully, Colonel," said Carstairs. "Absolutely. Best plan."

"And I," said Reville.

Witherspoon turned his gaze upon me.

"You flatter me, gentlemen, with your confidence," I said quietly. "But it is true that I know the country and understand the ways of the tribes thereabouts, and can treat with them in their own language, which may give me, as chance would have it, a slight edge with regard to the question of leadership."

I looked at Witherspoon and straightened my shoulders before his unblinking gaze.

"Thank you, sir," I said, "for making the suggestion. I willingly accept the burden of leadership. You may place your trust in me."

We joined hands, then, all four of us, as one does on the playing field.

"And with God's help," I said, "our mission will have a successful conclusion."

"With God's help," Carstairs and Reville echoed.

"Harrumph," Witherspoon added solemnly.

III
Mystery in Mombasa

I must confess that I always enjoy visiting Mombasa. It is true that it has its dangers—evil-eyed Arabs, sly Chinamen, smiling Punjabees, all of whom would run you through and leave your carcass at the bottom of a ditch in order to steal the shirt from your back—but they do give the place a sort of charm for the adventurer, I have always thought. And it is a wonderful place for hearing current news of what is happening in the world. Mombasa has been a bustling trading port for some thousands of years now, by all accounts, and the news there is seldom less than a fortnight old. Extraordinary place for news. It is less extraordinary for looks and convenience, of course, but then you can't have everything.

We sailed in toward Old Harbor, avoiding the swamps of Kilindini Harbor, and past Old Town with its white walls gleaming in the sun and a minaret sticking up above the rooftops. Terrible caterwauling the Arabians put up morning and night from those things, but of course the blighters don't know any better.

The details of docking and disembarking will be familiar to readers of these chronicles of the Club, so they may be dispensed with. Everything went in orderly fashion—remarkable, considering our distance from London—and, since it was still before noon, my companions and I determined to have a go at locating poor Berresford's last resting place before lunch.

The dock was lined with a motley assortment of locals. Once we four were assembled with our few belongings, I strode across to the gaping crowd—even in these days, four properly turned out English gentlemen still make a thrilling sight to those sorry beggars—and looked them over. At once, a young fellow separated himself from the others and came toward me. He was better-looking than the rest, cleaner, and straighter. A glance determined that he was the likeliest-looking of the lot.

"You there," I said. "Do you speak English?"

It was hard to tell from his looks what tribe had produced him, but I thought I detected a distant family resemblance to the Masai. This was strange, because the Masai never come to the city. In any event, he stood before me at once—a big fellow, nearly naked, but I thought I saw a gleam of intelligence and honesty in his eyes.

"Yes, Bwana," he said smartly. "I am at your service."

"Good, good," I said briskly. One must be businesslike with these fellows or they will think you less than a chief.

"My friends and I are going upcountry," I announced. "We shall need a headman to arrange for bearers, but first we wish to conduct some business in Mombasa. The man who can aid us in that and who shows himself to be honest and a willing worker will be first in our considerations for the position of headman."

"Yes, Bwana," the fellow said. "I am at your service."

"Good, very good," I said. I rubbed my hands together briskly as a sign of my impatience to get on with my affairs and my unwillingness to brook any nonsense. Gestures like that are a sort of *lingua franca* in the wilder parts of the world. A man can go far with a few carefully chosen and well-executed gestures.

"What is your name?" I asked the fellow.

To my surprise, I saw a look of hesitation in his face.

"You may call me by what name pleases you, Bwana," he said very quietly. There was some quality in his voice I could not make out.

"Well, never mind that for now," I said. "For the time being, you shall be called Number One. Do you understand? Your name is Number One, but only so long as you work hard. If you don't, then someone else shall be Number One. Is that clear?"

Number One nodded solemnly. These people have only two forms of facial expression, for the most part—either solemn or extremely gay—but they seem to feel this in no way limits them. One learns this sort of thing in dealing with the varied and colorful peoples of this wide world.

"Yes, Bwana," said the newly christened Number One.

"Well, then, Number One, pick out some of your friends there, enough to carry the things we have brought, and bring them along. But, here, the fellows you pick out must be"—I ticked off the points on my fingers—"strong, healthy, honest, and willing to work hard. When you have made your choices, bring them along and send the others away."

I had no sooner turned my back than Number One's crowd of friends set up an astonishingly loud palaver, all of them, I suppose, clamoring for the positions being dispensed. It was a good sign that those he selected would be willing to work hard later on.

When I rejoined my companions, Witherspoon said, "Harrumph."

"Yes," I said, "he looks like an honest fellow to me too. Well then, gentlemen, my idea is to visit at once the most important merchant of expeditionary stores in Mombasa, place our order, and then go in search of poor Berresford's grave whilst the provisions are being assembled."

The plan was agreed and, with Number One and some of his boys following with the baggage on their heads, we set off for the bazaar and the place of business of one Abdullah ben Achmed.

The heat, of course, was beastly, but we ignored it. I sometimes think that, in contrast, the cool temperatures and balmy breezes of England have contributed not a little to the advanced civilization of her people.

I had dealt with this Abdullah ben Achmed several times in years gone by. He was an unrepentant thief, of course, but he always had a better stock of provisions than anyone else in Mombasa, so there was nothing for it.

Our walk through the crowded streets of Mombasa drove home to us the fact that we were truly arrived in Africa. There were cries in a dozen languages, goods for sale from the four corners of the earth, and the air was redolent with the scent of a hundred spices. Ah, Africa!

When we were halfway to the bazaar, I directed Carstairs and Reville toward the place where the proposed railway station was being constructed. I don't suppose the line itself will be completed in this century—seems lions keep eating the Chinamen imported to work on it, or some such thing—but it makes a pleasant diversion for the natives. At any rate, I charged Carstairs and Reville with finding out what they could of poor Berresford or his headman, Jeremiah. There would be decent Englishmen there and one of them was sure to know something.

Witherspoon came along with me. We found Abdullah ben Achmed at his shop in the center of the bazaar. He recognized me at once, bright eyes darting in his swarthy Arabian face, and made a big salaam of welcome. Witherspoon discreetly waited outside while I wrangled for what we needed.

"Effendi!" Abdullah ben Achmed cried. "My heart is filled with gladness to see you once more and to see that you are well. Allah is good to you, for I see the years have left no mark."

"Never mind that," I told him. "I need food, provisions, stores, guns, the lot, enough for three weeks. We are going upcountry."

"Of course, Effendi," he said at once, rubbing his hands together at thoughts of the handsome—nay, extortionate—profit he would be raking in. "Everything shall be as you wish, Effendi; it is my greatest pleasure to serve you. And where is it that you go upcountry, Effendi?"

"Upcountry, Abdullah, that's all you need to know."

"But, Effendi," he said, "if I know where you are going, I can choose for you all the better." The fellow had moved closer to me and his teeth shone in his swarthy face like the fangs of a beast in the wild. When a man calls you "Effendi" and smiles, tread carefully.

"See here, Abdullah," I said, "I have told you what I want and there's an end of it. If your storehouses are empty, I will go elsewhere." This was impossible, of course, because Abdullah ben Achmed had long since murdered all his competition—the Arabian devil!—but saying it was part of the haggling on which these people dote.

"Effendi, of course it shall be my greatest pleasure in life to do all in my power to make the road before you stretch smoothly. Simply name your needs and it shall be done at the lowest possible price. I make you my solemn pledge that I shall give you a price so low that it shall surely impoverish me and send my children to beg in the bazaar, but for you, Effendi, I shall do this."

"Never mind that," I told him. Rob you blind, they will, if you let them. "Stores for three weeks, elephant guns, repeating rifles, pistols, four each, two hundred rounds of ammunition per gun. Have it ready in an hour."

"One hour, Effendi!" he cried. The villain actually contrived to look shocked. "Oh, Effendi, all this I shall provide for you, but to accomplish it I must send runners to the far corners of the city, many runners and many servants, all of whom rob me, the dogs, because they know I must act with speed. For this I am obliged to pay them extra, Effendi—"

"One hour," I said, and stared the fellow into silence. After a moment, defeated, he turned away and began snapping orders to his servants, who scurried off and disappeared among the stalls of the bazaar.

"Now, Abdullah, I wish to have a private word with you."

"Of course, Effendi, of course! It shall be my great pleasure to offer you hospitality."

While Witherspoon bought fruit in the bazaar for our noonday meal, Abdullah and I repaired to the back room of his shop.

"Abdullah," I said, "I want some information."

"Of course, Effendi. I sell more information than merchandise."

He smiled at once, showing me all his teeth. An absolutely wicked-looking fellow, but, it was true, he was the best source of information in Mombasa, had been for thirty years. If Abdullah ben Achmed didn't know where Berresford was buried, no one did.

I asked him.

I had never, in all our dealings over the years, seen the wily thief waver as he did when I told him what I needed to know. This was a man, it must be understood, who would sell his own children into slavery if you offered to pay in sterling, and here he was looking suddenly frightened at my question.

"I know nothing about it," he said. I instantly took note that he no longer addressed me with a title of respect.

"Abdullah," I said, feigning weariness, "we are two men of the world, you and me. We understand each other. I will pay for the information."

"I know nothing," he said, and his eyes refused to meet my own.

I asked repeatedly but the scoundrel only grew more uneasy and more insistent with each question. He flatly denied that he knew anything of Berresford's grave, and in fact pretended never to have heard of the dead man. And Berresford a member of the Club!

"That is the rankest nonsense, Abdullah. Absolute rubbish! You fitted him out yourself."

"I do not know the man," he said sullenly.

I switched my tactics and enquired after the native guide, Jeremiah, but the Arab stoutly insisted that he had never heard of such a person.

It was hopeless. Try as I might, I could get nothing from the fellow.

Finally, I stood up to leave.

"Effendi," Abdullah said, "do you go in search of this Englishman?"

I looked him straight in the eyes and he dropped his gaze at once.

Then, to my astonishment, he said, "Effendi, I am grieved to tell you this, but my memory is failing and I have only just remembered that the last of my stores was sold to an expedition of Germans only yesterday. I have nothing for you, nothing."

What in the name of God could have provoked a reaction like

this? Abdullah ben Achmed turning down a sale? Unheard-of behavior in his race.

There followed an animated conversation between us. Suffice it to say that it was only with the actual money, good English sterling coins, held up before his eyes, that the fellow at last relented. Even so, he was clearly not happy, and it was obvious that he wanted to see us on our way at the earliest possible instant. Snapping and snarling in that awful Arab tongue, he sent a new wave of servants scampering off after the first to hurry them along.

I stepped outside to think things over and confer with Witherspoon.

Clearly there was no chance of finding the grave. If Abdullah truly did not know, then neither did anyone else, including any Englishmen Carstairs and Reville might have questioned at the construction site. Or, what was worse, if Abdullah refused to tell me—for whatever arcane Arabian reasoning ruled his evil mind—then I strongly doubted that anyone else would tell us either, even if they knew.

But what troubled me even more was the fellow's steadfast refusal even to admit that he was acquainted with Berresford. This was a very bad sign, on which I could put only the darkest interpretation. One explanation, and one only, came to my mind, and that was related to Berresford's mention, in his letter, of a curse.

Now it must be understood that when the natives get on about a curse, it is a very serious thing to them and one must tread carefully. I have known talk of curses to be the downfall of more than one expedition, and not only on the African continent. Bearers run off in the night. Trusted boys betray you. That sort of thing. And sometimes, with the most threatening sort of native curse, silence is the first sign of danger. Abdullah was no black tribesman in the wild, of course, but the fear I saw in his eyes was the same I had seen on the faces of tribal chieftains, otherwise brave warriors, when faced with a local curse. Sometimes the fear can even be passed along to other peoples, and sometimes, even though rarely, it can be seen in villains like Abdullah. I didn't like it. I didn't like it at all.

I decided there and then that I would not ask Abdullah to provide bearers for us. Anyway, I didn't think the fellow would do it. We would have to rely on Number One and trust to Providence for the rest, but caution warned me not to tell Number One and his boys of our destination. I would have to warn the others to keep mum on the subject too, and not to speak poor Berresford's name aloud.

What is more, Abdullah did not invite us to have tea with him before departing. It was another very bad sign.

I joined Witherspoon outside just as Carstairs and Reville were returning. As I had expected, they had nothing to report. I whispered my instructions to them with a promise to explain fully later.

It was not long before the servants of Abdullah returned with the supplies we would need. The sad thought struck me that, only some months before, poor Berresford had stood in this very place, witnessing the very same scene, and possibly the girl with him. I wondered where she was now, but we would see, we would see. I shook the thoughts off.

I took Number One aside and told him that I trusted him—provisionally, of course—and that I wanted him to organize enough bearers to carry our stores. He understood at once and set about the task with a will. It seemed that some of his friends had followed us to the bazaar and were ready to hand. I counted eight of them, which I thought sufficient. Then I saw Number One approaching me again.

Speaking in Swahili, he asked, "The boys want to know where we are going, Bwana."

"That way," I said at once in the same language, and pointed inland from the sea. "And when we arrive where we are going—and, mind you, not a day before—I shall pay them their wages. Tell them that."

Number One proved his usefulness immediately in silencing what protest they might have made.

By then, our stores were piled in the dust at our feet, we had slaked our hunger and thirst both with fruit from the bazaar, and the bearers were ready and waiting to lift their burdens.

Abdullah was waiting to be paid, but even the prospect of that did nothing to lift his spirits. Even more to my amazement—my utter amazement, I should say—he did not even protest when I handed him what I knew to be the correct and fair price.

"Well, then, Abdullah," I said, "that concludes our business."

He offered no blessing on our journey, which is customary among his people, so I turned on my heel and started from the shop.

"Effendi," he said softly as I reached the doorway.

I turned to face him.

"Some peoples in this land," he said quietly, "cherish death as much as life. Some peoples in this land call Kilimanjaro 'the grave of strangers.' If you go there, soon you will be in the presence of Allah. I envy you for that, Effendi, but I also fear for you."

His words, obviously torn from him after a violent inner struggle, made the blood run like ice water in my veins. Even the baking noonday heat of Mombasa could do nothing to warm it.

IV
An Attack in the Night

Once we were out of the town itself, we set off in a north-north-westerly direction. Kilimanjaro lies two hundred miles or so to the northwest of Mombasa, but I thought it best to conceal our destination from the bearers until we were several days' trekking from the town. As it turned out, this proved to be a good plan.

There was nothing to guide us but a compass and the equatorial sun. Primitive place, Africa, lacking facilities for any sort of civilized existence, although I expect that Englishmen will change all that in the decades to come. For the first few hours out of Mombasa we had the luxury of a dirt track to follow, but then we were on our own in the bush.

The bush. No one who has not seen the interior of Africa can imagine it, although in writing "the bush" I mean thereby a considerably varied landscape. The bush may be burning desert, scrub-dotted plain, tangled and steaming jungle, or impenetrable forest. Where we were going, we expected to encounter them all.

Africa is blessed with a wonderfully rich soil in places, even where it doesn't look promising. All it wants is a back not afraid to bend and a little old-fashioned English persistence.

Witherspoon commented on this when Mombasa was some four hours behind us and we stopped to boil some water for tea. We were sitting on our little camp chairs, not talking much, saving our breath for our exertions, when he sat up straighter and looked all round us in a sweeping circle. The plain was dotted with thick, squat baobab trees, the occasional flame tree, and the shadow tree or acacia.

"Harrumph!" he said emphatically, and waved an arm at the vast expanse. Then he leaned forward and scrabbled a bit in the dirt at our feet. Beneath the crisp, sun-heated surface was a rich black soil. He held up a handful for our examination. "Harrumph," he said, with a mixture of sadness and longing.

"It is a pity, Colonel," I said. "Waste, all waste. It is a garden, indeed, but only *in potentia*. My God, just think of the blooms this soil and climate would make possible."

Both he and I cultivated roses at home and shared many interesting conversations on the subject. He shook his head sadly at the impossibility of it all, and then resignedly pushed himself to his feet and said, "Harrumph."

He was right. We had more pressing purposes in mind just at the moment. It was time to push onward. We still had nearly two good hours of daylight before the abrupt African evening would wrap us in darkness.

We pitched camp that first night near a dry riverbed. We had spotted no game within shooting distance all afternoon—confounded bad luck, first time in my experience—and had to make do with tinned goods. Still, the tea was strong and bracing, once I explained to Number One the proper way of making it. After our meal we wasted no time in crawling between our blankets, for the African nights can be cool in those regions—a pleasant homelike touch, I have always thought—and dropping into a profound sleep almost at once.

But barely had we drifted into pleasant dreams of England than we were awakened by a sound I have often heard in the African bush, and which never fails to rouse me in an instant from the deepest slumber. In that, I have developed the instincts of a native. It was the coughing of a lion. The sound came from downwind of our camp, which meant the beast knew of our presence.

Without rising, I turned my head and saw that Witherspoon, old trekker that he was, had awakened too.

From nearby, Number One whispered, "Simba, Bwana." His voice was so low that it might have been nothing more than the stirring of a breeze in the grass.

Good fellow, I thought, alert and ready for any danger. I was to learn that very night exactly how brave a fellow Number One would prove to be.

We listened without moving or rousing the others, and heard the lion cough again. On the hunt, I thought, and an old fellow, judging from the sound of him—old and wily, an experienced hunter who had survived many seasons.

For the moment, however, there was nothing to do but lie still and attract no more attention than we had already, while keeping track of his distance and direction by the sounds he made.

With stealthy movements, Witherspoon and I drew our rifles to our sides and got them into position ready for a quick shot.

Nothing in the world matches the experience of lying on the African plain, the air filled with the scents of exotic flora, the moon a disk of silver and the stars shining brightly high above in the black night sky, all your muscles relaxed but at the ready, your senses honed to razor sharpness, ears alert to the slightest sound, while you wait for a hungry lion to strike.

After some little while, however, we heard the old killer's coughing grow fainter and fainter and finally disappear altogether. He had gone off, it seemed. Perhaps he had picked up the scent of likelier game, giraffe or eland or kudu. We listened carefully but there was not a sound to indicate his presence.

After some brief whispering among ourselves, so as not to disturb our fellows, the three of us settled in once again to sleep.

It was about an hour later that the lion attacked.

The wily beast, his natural intelligence improved by perhaps three decades of hunting experience, had not gone in pursuit of other game. Indeed, we should have realized this—I felt it was a serious lapse of cautious leadership on my part, and duly offered my apologies afterward, and naturally make no show of concealing my error in this factual account—for we ourselves, as it chanced, had spotted no game in all the miles we had crossed in the afternoon. This is unusual but it can happen, and the lion, wishing to feed, had settled on us as his only prey. He had indeed gone off as we had thought, but this was only to fool us. He had then circled round to approach his target from another quarter, one in which we would not expect to find him. All this we determined only afterward, of course.

He came at us like a very demon out of Hell, mad for the taste of human blood.

The first I knew, one of the bearers screamed in terror and agony as the beast tore him with savage fangs. Then, in a second, all the bearers were screaming as the rest of us flung our blankets aside and leaped to our feet, snatching at our guns. There was no possibility of bringing the rifles into play at such close quarters. In a second the situation was clear, and we had to back off rapidly as the ravening beast turned in our direction. To my horror, I saw it advance, dragging the lifeless body of a second bearer in its jaws, to the very spot where our loaded pistols lay on the ground. We were defenseless, and the beast, driven to a savage frenzy by the smell of blood, would not stop now until each and every one of us lay dead.

To our horror, the animal now turned his attention to Carstairs and Reville, as if picking them out deliberately as its next victims. In a second it had hurled itself at poor Carstairs, who had no time even to raise a hand before the beast had torn out his throat. And in another second the same lot had befallen Reville. I was revolted by the spectacle—our campsite was now a scene of bloody carnage in the moonlight—and all the more so knowing that Witherspoon and I, frozen where we stood, would meet the same fate in a moment's time. It would do no good, we knew, to imitate the surviving bearers, who had run off into the night, for the beast would only hunt us down and kill us one by one.

The beast turned its bloodstained face to Witherspoon and myself. Even by moonlight, I thought I could see the bloodlust in its eyes.

"By Jove!" Witherspoon breathed at my ear, and I thought never to hear his kindly voice again.

"Long live England and the Queen!" I breathed. I felt Witherspoon squeeze my arm.

And it was in that very instant that we witnessed an astonishing sight.

As we faced the beast that we knew must shortly devour us, we saw Number One rise up from the darkness and hurl himself on the animal's back. The blade of a knife flashed for an instant in the moonlight, and then Number One, clinging to the beast's mane for dear life with one hand, used the other to plunge the blade into the animal's throat. The beast roared with fury and flung itself about like a thing demented, which indeed it was, but Number One clung there, sinking the knife again and again, seeking a vital spot. We knew the native's plan could not succeed, for in an instant the beast would fling him away and tear him limb from limb, but tears sprang into our eyes nevertheless at his noble attempt to save us.

And yet Number One clung there on the back of the lion and none of the beast's mad twistings and turnings could shake him free. The animal's roarings were fearful to hear, but shortly it coughed, then coughed again with a bubbling sound. It trembled violently and then we heard the unmistakable sound of its death rattle. Number One's thrusting blade had done its work.

The beast was dead and silence once again filled the night. The only sound was the labored, ragged breathing of Number One, who had rolled free and now lay on his back in a pool of the lion's blood.

Never otherwise in my life had I been privileged to witness such a spectacle of bravery and prowess performed by an African.

"By Jove!" Witherspoon exclaimed. I could not have felt more strongly about it myself, or expressed it better.

We rushed to the fellow's side to determine if he had suffered any injuries. As we took hold of him and set him on his feet, we heard the remaining bearers cautiously returning after their flight. We could not blame them for fleeing, the poor terrified blighters, and now we saw in their shining eyes the same admiration we felt ourselves for Number One.

I put my hand on the fellow's shoulder and spoke a heartfelt, "Thank you."

Beside me, Witherspoon placed a hand on the fellow's other shoulder and, shaking his head in wonder, cleared his throat and spoke his most emphatic "Harrumph!"

It was the highest tribute he could pay, and it expressed my own feelings exactly.

V

A Sad Dawn

It was with mixed emotions that our little party set out the next morning from that first night's camp.

The night itself had brought little rest, for following the lion's savage attack none of us, not even the bearers, had been able to sleep soundly. While I tossed and turned myself, dozing only fitfully, I could hear the others doing the same. No doubt the dreadful thoughts that assailed them were identical to my own. We had all lost dear and lifelong friends in the attack.

Poor Carstairs and Reville—both dead, and not yet twenty-four hours in Africa! Apart from the shock I felt at their lives being cut off in their prime, at the grief that news of their deaths would bring to the Club, I felt most keenly the loss of fellow adventurers, brave men of my own temperament, unblinking in the face of danger but brought down by the sheer and unpredictable savagery of nature untamed. True, every member of the Club knows that such a fate might befall him at any moment on an expedition such as this, and we had all, I think, resigned ourselves to the possibility, but can one ever be fully prepared for death? Such speculations robbed me of sleep through the remainder of that grim and unforgettable night.

And with the first sharp light of dawn, which comes as abruptly as evening in these latitudes, the first sight that greeted our eyes was the hideous scene of carnage that the night had partly obscured in shadow. We had dragged away to a little distance the mangled remains of Carstairs and Reville and the two bearers, and then dragged to a greater distance the bloody body of the lion. Now, by the harsh light of day, we discovered that our toll of casualties was even higher, for we found yet another one of the bearers whom apparently the lion had ripped open casually in passing, perhaps even while the man still slept. We prayed that was the case and that he'd been spared the sight of his killer, as the other victims had not. Shaking our heads in silent wonder and renewed grief, we carried his body away and laid it beside the others. Five men dead, killed violently within a matter of seconds. It was a sobering thought.

We worked in silence, for the most part, only pointing and murmuring the occasional quiet word, as we dug a pit and reverently laid the five bodies in the bottom of it. When the pit was filled in, I set the natives to scouring the area for some rocks large enough to set atop the grave to discourage jackals from digging up the remains, for in Africa, perhaps more than in any other part of the globe, life will readily feed upon death.

It was sad work. When it was done, I murmured a quiet prayer and Witherspoon, his voice hoarse with emotion, muttered a grieving "Harrumph." The remaining bearers had no ceremony to honor their fallen comrades, but I had no doubt, from their solemn expressions, that they felt the loss as sharply as did Witherspoon and I. At any rate, that was a question I had ample opportunity to contemplate in the weeks to come.

Now, with our complement of servants thus dramatically reduced —there remained only five bearers, plus the headman, Number One

—it was necessary for Witherspoon and myself to reformulate our plans. I called Number One to my side to take part in the discussion.

Carefully weighing the utility of each item, we determined which and how much of the stores we had could be taken with us. These were hard decisions. While it was true, for example, that we now needed to carry less water, it was also true that we had fewer men to carry the essentials—weapons, ammunition, knives, medical supplies, digging tools, cooking implements, dried foodstuffs, a chest of cut black Ceylon, a case of brandy, glass and copper beads for trading.

Number One proved very useful in advising on these decisions. I noted that, while his manner was suitably reserved in light of the night's tragedy, he was making a heroic effort to conceal the pain his wounds must have brought him. At the same time, he was clearly pleased with the deep scars those same wounds must perforce leave permanently on his chest and arms and face. Now, unlike most African warriors, he would never need to boast. The scars would betoken his courage for all the world to see. The worst of them were on his chest, which had nearly been laid open to the ribs, and I surmised—correctly, I think—that if this fellow were magically set down in the middle of Piccadilly in January, nothing would induce him to don a shirt.

And so, dispirited and saddened by our losses, and wearied by our lack of proper rest, we resumed our journey once again, moving ever deeper into Africa's mysterious interior.

VI
Across the Plain and into the Jungle

We were, I expect, a rather sorry-looking spectacle, had there been anyone in the region to study our appearance, and it needs must be that we grew sorrier still, in both outward aspect and inward attitude, with every day that passed.

The weather was beastly, with ever more scorching days and ever colder nights. We would have traveled by night, as one must in some of the world's climes and as I myself have often done, sheltering as best one can by day from the direct rays of the sun, but the roughness of the terrain here ruled out that possibility. It was treacherous land, rocky and uneven. One felt that the vultures occasionally sighted floating high above were only waiting to see an ankle turned painfully on a stone. There were sudden slopes, riverbeds dry since primordial times, a million places to put a foot wrong. There was nothing for it. Despite heat that seemed to sear one's very lungs, we must perforce travel by day.

The days seemed both endless—at noon, the cool of evening seemed nothing more than a fantasy dreamed in delirium—and countless in their numbers. Day followed day as weary footstep followed weary footstep. We stumbled, we coughed in the dust of our own slow passage, we baked in the sun; still, benumbed as we were, we stumbled forward.

It was a struggle sometimes to keep my thoughts from wandering out of control, just as it was a struggle to keep my feet moving steadily forward. But duty compelled me: duty to Carstairs and Reville, who lay behind us to enrich the African soil with their bones; duty to Witherspoon, whose greater age made him now more dependent on my leadership; duty to myself, for I had sworn a solemn vow to complete my mission; duty to England—how could it be otherwise?—and duty to the Adventurers Club and to the honor of its courageous members in whatever farflung corners of the world they might find themselves.

And two further obligations impelled me as well. Though it would be sacrilege to call them higher duties than those I have just enumerated, yet can I say that they were as forceful, at least, as the others.

First, poor Berresford had sent the Club a cry for help, a cry that must be answered, and which *had* been answered by our instant departure from London. Our duty there was being discharged. Still, Berresford himself was dead. So much for him.

The other obligation was the goal, the very heart and lifeblood, of our quest. An Englishwoman was in distress and needed rescuing. What obligation could be clearer?

As we trudged across endless dusty miles beneath the burning African sun, thoughts of the girl filled my mind. We did not know who she was, or what she looked like. We did not even know her name. But if, when we found her—as find her we would—she was still alive to be saved, we would save her. There could be no question of that.

Thinking closely on this goal was, I found, marvelously refreshing and helped wonderfully to clarify my thoughts.

Indeed, I had much to think about. Witherspoon, who until now had been a source of wise advice to me at every step, began to show the effects of our endless exertions. His speech was now limited to a hoarse and choking "Harrumph," and even that put a strain on his voice.

I was alone. In my extremity, I came to rely more and more upon the advice of the intrepid Number One, whom I now permitted to walk at my side, except, of course, for when we had to urge the bearers on to greater efforts.

I could see the growing concern in Number One's dark eyes, for the bearers grew wearier with every step, and more apprehensive as well.

By the third day, Kilimanjaro had come into view in the distance on our left. It is a magnificent sight, one of the finest this world has to offer, its peaks ringed by white clouds, its slopes rising majestically from the plain without benefit of foothills. But we were not travelers on holiday, far from it, and the mountain's beauties, at least until our mission should be accomplished, were lost on us.

I had noticed, from time to time, one or another of the bearers casting a fearful look to the south, toward the mountain. Even the usual look of steadfast determination in Number One's dusky features was occasionally clouded over when he glanced in that direction. For these reasons, I kept my own counsel and only gradually steered our path in a curve that would eventually bring us to Kilimanjaro. It meant perhaps two extra days of walking—a daunting prospect, I will admit—but seemed better than alarming the superstitious natives prematurely.

But I have frequently found it to be the case that primitive peoples, no matter how benighted their minds may be with regard to civilized behavior, are guided by some inner light or instinct—call it native intelligence,* if you will—that leads them on the safest path through the wilderness of dangers one may encounter in a lifetime.

So it was with our boys. A suspicion grew in their minds of what our real goal was, and it was only with constant vigilance that Number One could silence their murmurings.

---

* Sir Clive seems unaware here of the punning effect of his words. It is unlikely that he intended the effect; such levity would not be in keeping with his nature. —*Editor*

It was only by the luckiest chance that their worries were, at least temporarily, laid to rest. On the very day I fully expected them to lay down their burdens and refuse to go a step farther, we spotted a small herd of elephant, perhaps fifteen or twenty. Fortunately, we were downwind of the beasts or they would have been off in a flash.

I signaled the others to lie flat on the ground while I took one of the big guns and Number One and I crawled cautiously closer. I picked out a big bull—the tusks must have weighed nearly fifty pounds apiece. I have ever afterward regretted having to leave them; how they would have adorned the Reading Room—and sighted carefully for a shot to the brain. I should only have the one chance, for a miss would scatter the brutes instantly to the four points of the compass.

Well, I got him, and the huge beast struck the earth with a heavy thud while his fellows scattered across the plain, trumpeting their fright.

The bearers were instantly mad with joy, and came running forward, knives at the ready, looking for all the world like the bloodthirsty savages they can be when they forget themselves or find themselves in some extremity.

But, in a way, I could understand their relief, for the truth was that I felt much the same thing myself, and I know that Witherspoon, weary as he was, did too.

Here, at a stroke, we were provided with delicious food—in a week, we had taken only one eland and a baby giraffe, with hardly enough meat on him to make a meal—together with entertainment, employment, excitement, and a wonderful change from the daily routine.

It was nearing evening when I shot the beast, so I gave orders to make camp there and then. Even the time was with us, for the cool evening would not spoil the meat as quickly as would the heat of day. Elephant steaks and the wonderful, rich heart of the beast. Yes, I shared the natives' excitement. Soon the bearers, wielding their knives with familiar authority, were pulling back the skin and carving off the best of the meat. In minutes, they were stained red from head to toe with the animal's blood, and grinning like children engaged in the most delightful play.

To make our joy even greater, Number One discovered, about a hundred yards from where the elephant had fallen, a narrow trickle of water that somehow avoided sinking into the thirsty earth. We were closer to Kilimanjaro now, and would be finding more water, borne down the slopes from its snow-capped top, from here on. The present fortuitous find compounded our immediate pleasure.

There is nothing like a change of pace, a hearty meal, and an extra hour's sleep to dispel fear, I always say, and so it proved that night. Each and every one of us slept like a babe, secure in the knowledge that our own deaths had been held at bay for at least one day longer.

And the next day, with Witherspoon and myself feeling stronger and clearer-headed, with the bearers anxious but still willing to go forward, Number One suddenly raised an arm and pointed forward. A dark line of green shimmered before us.

We had reached the jungle. For the time being, at least, we were saved.

VII

A Morning in the Jungle

The reader who has never personally experienced the African jungle can never adequately imagine the reality of the thing. Even so, I am forced to wonder if perhaps, in the end, it is only the power of the imagination that can properly capture the equatorial jungle, for words seem poor things indeed with which to describe it in all its variety.

It is no neatly trimmed and well-behaved St. James's Park, you may be sure. Rather, it is a hothouse that has been permitted to run amok. The trees soar to dizzying heights, blocking out the sun in places; the flowers, where the sunlight penetrates, grow to gigantic proportions in colors that beggar the vocabulary to describe. Above one's head birds dart, sending out their calls, and small mammals dash about on their myriad purposes, using the branches as boulevards. Monkeys chatter at one's passing. And beneath the feet, the earth itself is buried in a moist and spongy compost of decay, and every step sends up a misty cloud of vapor.

After the dry and burning heat of the plains, the moist and shady jungle seemed a very heaven sent to comfort us.

Upon reaching it, I gave the order that we would not penetrate its depths but rather stay near the edge, taking once more the opportunity to rest ourselves. The bearers were sent in search of food and water. Presently they returned, their arms laden with succulent fruits and with word that a stream ran swift and clear not a hundred paces away. Then two of them fashioned spears from a couple of straight tree branches. They disappeared into the jungle and not twenty minutes later returned with the carcass of a small wild pig. Elephant steak the night before, roast pork tonight!

Our pleasure, alas, was short-lived, as I had known in my innermost thoughts it would be—thoughts I had rejected for a while in favor of a temporary pleasure and relief. It is foolish to do so, of course, but nearly impossible to resist, for nature beguiles the weary adventurer by magnifying any boon.

When we awoke in the morning, after a night's jungle symphony of bird calls and raucous animal cries, we found that the baking heat of the plains had been replaced by a heat that would now, it seemed, boil us to death in the juice of our own tortured bodies.

"Harrumph," Witherspoon said in discomfort. I felt the same way, as if the very blood were boiling in my veins.

Oddly, though, the jungle climate worked to our advantage in one way.

Number One, I saw from the first moment I awoke, was holding an animated palaver with the bearers, who were once again, it seemed, refusing to go forward. Then, after some agreement had apparently been reached, Number One made his way along the bank of the little stream and approached Witherspoon and myself where we were standing.

In a moment, Number One had made the situation clear. The boys were all from a tribe, he explained, that lived in the coolest part of the highlands. The heat of the plains was wearisome to them on a long trek such as ours, but far from devastating. But the humid heat of the jungle seemed to them now nearly unbearable. Upon awaking, they had announced to him their wish to leave the jungle at once. Number One, employing the marvelous diplomacy of which he seemed endlessly capable, had somehow persuaded them not to go backward, across the plains we had just traversed. Rather, they were now willing to go forward, it appeared, through the jungles at the foot of Mount Kilimanjaro and upward a little distance to where the jungle once again died out, where the air was cooler, where the water ran freely down the slopes, and where the game was plentiful and easily taken.

I could not imagine what argument Number One could have made to them, for I had heard the boys whispering in the night, frightening each other further—or so I thought—with their own terrifying superstitions about what would happen to those who trespassed on Mount Kilimanjaro. It had been my intention to discuss this with Number One immediately upon awaking, but it appeared that he had already solved the problem by his own cleverness. I once again congratulated myself on choosing him as headman.

"Number One," I said, "are they not afraid of the gods and spirits of the mountain?"

"They are, Bwana," he answered. I thought his features were set in a very solemn expression. Yet, some excitement I could not identify seemed to lurk in his eyes. "But, Bwana, I tell you they will go forward and climb the mountain willingly."

"I had expected otherwise. Why is this, Number One? What have you said to them?"

"I have shown them good reason, Bwana," Number One said gravely, and his gaze boldly met my own. There was nothing of impudence in it, only a degree of confidence that I had long suspected in the man and that now was bearing its richest fruit. It was obvious that the fellow had known all along what our true destination was, but since I had kept silent about it, he had done likewise. I thought it best to say nothing of this aloud, but I determined that, the instant we emerged at the other side of the belt of jungle and faced the true slopes of Kilimanjaro, I would take him fully into my confidence and explain the exact nature of the task that lay ahead.

But I could not keep myself from putting one further question to him.

"Number One," I said, "you say that the boys fear the spirits of the mountain, yet they will go forward. Tell me this. Are you afraid yourself, or are you a man completely without fear?"

He looked at me a long time before he answered. When at last he spoke, his reply was not a little surprising.

"Bwana," he said, "I speak truthfully to you. I fear only those things which make me afraid."

And with that, he turned away and went back to organize the bearers for the day's march.

Behind me, I heard Witherspoon's thoughtful "Harrumph."

VIII
Morning on the Mountain

The jungle was hellish, its heat stealing air from our lungs, its moisture soaking us through and through. The poor natives, accustomed to a more congenial climate, suffered like pygmies in a blizzard. There was little talking among any of us as we hacked and pushed our way through the tangled vegetation. The only thing that kept us going through that awful day was a sensation of the ground rising ever so slightly beneath our feet as we pressed onward. As difficult as it was to discern, we were going uphill. We were on the mountain. We had reached Kilimanjaro at last.

I had much to occupy my thoughts now, and my cogitations, confused and uncertain as they were, helped distract me a little from the heat and discomfort of the jungle.

I should have to talk with Number One, of course, and explain our mission to him. If need be, I would have to find a means of persuading him to remain in our service. Yet, I had the feeling that Number One had some secret of his own. I might almost have thought that secret was in the nature of a mission too. Only time would tell, of course, but there was one thing I knew for a certainty. I knew that Number One was the bravest African I had ever met.

Now that I was actually treading upon the soil of Kilimanjaro, the strange behavior, and the even stranger warning, of Abdullah ben Achmed came back vividly to my mind. What could he have been thinking? What could have frightened him so much, and he not a man easily frightened at all? He had been many years in Mombasa, had dealt with all sorts of cutthroats, was indeed a cutthroat himself. Could he have been so badly frightened by the ignorant talk of natives about a curse? Could some savage superstition do this to him? It seemed hard to believe, yet, for the time being, there could be no other explanation.

And then I thought—as I had never stopped thinking, really—of poor Berresford and the girl. On the morrow we would have to make our plans and then set about combing the mountainsides for signs of her. We should have to hope for an encounter with the tribes who lived on the mountain, while at the same time dreading any such meeting. It was a daunting prospect.

These thoughts occupied me fully throughout that day in the jungle. When night came we merely collapsed, every one of us, and fell into the deep sleep of exhaustion.

But the worst of our travels, at least, were at an end. When I woke in the morning, I found Number One standing over me. I was shocked to see him grinning, and rose hastily to my feet.

"Bwana," he explained, "I have scouted ahead. The jungle is at an end, no more than the half of a mile from here, and the mountain itself lies ahead."

I could not get over the way he was smiling, something I had never seen him do before, and asked him if there was some reason for his happiness other than our having passed through the belt of jungle.

His smile broadened at my question. "I know what I know, Bwana," was his only reply.

We broke camp quickly, all of us eager to escape the steaming clutches of the jungle. Number One willingly led the way. Within half an hour the vegetation grew more sparse, the trees lower and less luxuriant, and the ground beneath our feet more solid, and then suddenly—Oh, what a wonder it seemed!—a breeze brushed cooling fingers across my brow. Witherspoon sighed happily beside me and the bearers actually burst into delighted laughter.

Panting with eagerness, we broke out of the jungle and hurried up a long, gradual slope. The ground was covered with low, coarse vegetation, interspersed with crimson bougainvillea and thick, grayish cacti that raised twisted arms toward the wonderfully blue heavens above.

At the top of the slope we halted and stared in wonder at the spectacle that lay before us. We had climbed, it seemed, higher than we had thought, and now, spread out in every direction for our delight, arrayed in shades of green and ocher, was a living map of what appeared to be the whole eastern half of the African continent.

So beautiful was the sight that a strange and disturbing thought leaped at once into my mind. If ever there were an earthly abode of the gods, I thought—always excepting England, naturally enough—then surely Kilimanjaro must be it.

IX
A Conversation with Number One

Never, I thought, did a cup of morning tea taste so fresh and delightful as in the clean, clear air of the mountain. Even so, I did not linger long, for I wished to have a private little chat with Number One. I caught his eye and we strolled together some little distance away where we could not be overheard. Conveniently, we found two great flat rocks where we were able to seat ourselves. For the seeming luxury of it, we might have been in the Reading Room of the Club, although a half-naked savage would have raised some eyebrows there, I daresay.

"Number One," I began when we were settled, "I have much to say to you."

"And I have an equal number to say to you, Bwana."

"Yes, well, I rather expected that," I replied, and lifted an eyebrow at him, as much as to say, don't try to fool an Englishman, it can't be done.

"I would like to tell you a story, Bwana," Number One said. There was suddenly a deadly earnestness in his manner that could not be denied.

"Go ahead, then," I said.

I settled myself comfortably on the stone and prepared to listen.

"My name," he began, "is Ngugi wa Babatunde,* although most men in Mombasa, both white and black, know me as Henry.† This is because I have concealed my true name until today. The only others who know my identity are those"—he nodded toward the bearers, who were squatting near the fire and watching us, I was certain, from the corners of their eyes—"for they are half-brothers to me, as were the three who died by the claws and fangs of Simba, the lion god.

* It appears here that Sir Clive may have misheard Number One's name. "Ngugi" is common enough in eastern Africa, but "Babatunde" is a name more frequently associated with the region of the Niger River. —*Editor*
† The name "Henry" is frequently adopted by the Negroes of eastern Africa. The reason for this is not known. —*Editor*

"I must tell you something further. This name I have revealed to you is a great one, for it is the name of a king among my own people, the wa-Chagga."

I started at that, even more than at the heart of his announcement.

"The wa-Chagga!" I cried. "But are they not the wild and savage people who inhabit the mountain and drive all others away with their talk of curses and death?"

"They are," Number One, or Ngugi wa Babatunde, replied calmly, "but I tell you that they are not a savage and bloodthirsty people. They are strong, but they are gentle. They love peace as much as an Englishman loves peace, and they love Kilimanjaro as much as an Englishman loves England. I speak in this manner so that my meaning will be clear to you."

I was shocked by his words and had to catch my breath before replying.

"Number One—Ngugi, I mean—how is it that you are a king? And how is it that you do not rule over your people?"

"I am king because my father was king before me. I do not rule my people because I have been the victim of treachery, the treachery of one who I am ashamed to say is my own brother, who now wrongfully rules in my place.

"This is how it happened.

"My brother and I are twins, although we do not share the same face or stature. This can happen at times, and in the history of my family, the royal family of the wa-Chagga, it has happened in every other generation and has been the source of much fighting and bloodshed.

"My brother's name is Kamala. When Kamala and I were ten years of age, our father died of a sickness in his chest. Since I was the firstborn of his two sons, I was the one who should have been made king. But my brother, who was always bigger and stronger than I, and of a more warlike disposition, had been approached by greedy men among my father's retainers, who saw in my father's death an opportunity to win power for themselves. They wished to make Kamala the king rather than myself because they saw in him and his cruel ways a reflection of the evil in themselves.

"So I was cast out from my people. I was not killed by Kamala's men because that would have roused the anger of all, but I, and my eight half-brothers with me, were taken in hand and carried in bonds from the sacred mountain and left to die in the burning plains.

"But I did not die. And now I am bound to return to Kilimanjaro, to the sacred and ancestral home of my people, to rid them of the scourge of Kamala and return to them a world of peace."

For all that Number One, or Ngugi, spoke with determination, and certainly with the powers of oratory that seem to come so easily to African chieftains, this was clearly a very moving moment for him, as it was for me. This terrible tale of treachery and his own disinheritance had been bottled up within him for a decade, and was only now finding release.

"Tell me, Number One—" I began, but I was interrupted.

"Please," he said, "I would ask only two things of you. The first is that you cease calling me Number One. Please call me Ngugi. It is a mark of favor for me to invite this."

As I had noted with him before, this was no impudence on his part, merely an expression of his sense of his own place in the peculiar African scheme of things.

"Yes, well, of course," I said. "I shall be glad to. And please do you call me Waterstone-Foyle. I think that should balance things out nicely, don't you? But what is the other thing you wish to ask?"

"I will tell you that shortly," he replied.

"Tell me this, then," I said. "How is it that you and your half-brother hang about the docks in Mombasa and agree to work for white chiefs from across the water when you yourself are a chief?"

"That is a good question, Waterstone-Foyle," he said. He was silent a second, but I saw that his dark eyes were positively gleaming. "I have been waiting. I have been waiting for just such a man as yourself, one in whom I saw the same degree of courage and perseverance that I feel within myself. With such a man, my half-brothers and I could make the wearisome journey to Kilimanjaro and, with your aid, win back my rightful place among the wa-Chagga. That is the second thing I would ask of you, Waterstone-Foyle. Will you help me? I am a chief, but I ask this thing humbly."

"Well, that's all right, that's all right," I said hastily. "Of course I shall help you, and Witherspoon too, of course. I mean, after all, what's a chap to do, isn't that so?"

Ngugi, Number One that had been, bowed his head in dignified acknowledgment of my pledge to help. Then he raised his head and his eyes met mine.

"And what is it you would ask of me, Waterstone-Foyle?"

I cleared my throat and, without further preamble, told him that Witherspoon and myself and our lost colleagues were all members of the Adventurers Club, with quarters in Pall Mall—I could see that this impressed him—and that we were here on a mission no less sacred than his own.

I told him of poor Berresford's letter and I could see that he was saddened at news of our friend's death. But when I told him of Berresford's ward, a defenseless young Englishwoman who, even as we spoke, might be in danger of her life, or worse, at the hands of the very same evil men who had deposed their rightful king, a terrible anger suffused the dusky countenance of Ngugi.

"Will you help us find her and fetch her out safely, so that she may return to her own people, just as you wish to return to yours?" I concluded.

Ngugi rose at that and placed one hand upon my shoulder. I rose too and placed my own hand on one of his shoulders.

"Waterstone-Foyle," he said, "your task and mine, I think, are one and the same. Let us go forward together."

It was an emotional moment for both of us—I for one shall never forget it—and we stood in silence for several seconds. But talk was now a luxury with urgent business to be seen to.

"Our first step, then," I said, "will be to locate the wa-Chagga. What is the best way to do that?"

"It is not a step we need concern ourselves with, Waterstone-Foyle," Ngugi replied quietly. "Do not worry about it, for the wa-Chagga have already found us."

I looked past him then and was horrified to see a circle of warriors closing in about our little campsite on the mountain. They were tall and very dark-skinned, and their faces were painted like hideous masks. Each wore a necklace of lion's teeth and brandished a spear before him. As they came closer and ringed us in, all the while scowling fiercely, I thought I had never seen a more bloodthirsty and savage lot of wogs in all my days.

X
Prisoners!

There was not even the opportunity to offer resistance, futile though it must have been, and within minutes the savages had taken hold of us and were marching us off to their stronghold.

For that first half hour following our capture, the worst suffering we had to endure was the inability to speak to one another, for the savages had separated us, four men holding each as we walked. I could hear, somewhere behind me, Witherspoon's angry "Harrumph" as the brutes manhandled him, but I could offer nothing that would buck up his spirits. I devoted myself instead to heartfelt prayers that we would all be cast in together when we reached our place of imprisonment.

To my great relief, this turned out to be the case. Ngugi, his five half-brothers, Witherspoon, and I were roughly pushed through the narrow doorway of a rude hut, and eight warriors, one in honor of each of us, were posted outside to prevent our escape.

But at least we were together; there was that to be grateful for.

All eight of us were stunned by the suddenness of our imprisonment. What would become of us now? Were all our efforts to be for naught?

We were silent for some seconds. Then I turned toward Ngugi, who was surely our expert now in these matters.

"What will they do, Ngugi?" I whispered.

Ngugi was already crawling toward the entrance of the hut. He did not reply, but crouched there listening to the idle chatter of the guards outside. Their speech, I could tell, was a dialect of the Masai tongue, one that was strange to me, but I could make out about half of what they said. But I could tell from his expression that Ngugi understood every word.

"Harrumph," Witherspoon grunted in frustration, and the Lord knows I shared his feelings.

Finally Ngugi crawled away from the entrance and sat back on his haunches before Witherspoon and me. He gestured his half-brothers to come closer, and we formed a little circle.

"Kamala has been informed that his warriors have captured intruders. Intruders! That is what they call us . . ."

He had to stop speaking and calm himself before continuing.

"He will not see us yet, for he is readying himself at the moment for a great celebration to be held this very night. Kamala has declared that the gods of Kilimanjaro have accepted him as one of them. At tonight's ceremony, he will declare himself *to be a god!*"

"By Jove!" Witherspoon cried out, so loudly that one of the guards stuck his head in at the door and snarled something in his native tongue.

When we were alone again, Ngugi added, speaking even more softly than before, "There is something else unpleasant that I must tell you, and it is this. Kamala means to celebrate his assumption of godliness by taking a new wife, one of a sort never seen before among the wa-Chagga. I very much fear, Waterstone-Foyle, that we have found the object of your search, for the wife Kamala means to take is a woman who comes from a faraway land . . . and who has a skin as white as your own."

"Gad!" Witherspoon exploded, leaping to his feet. "Gad! Gad! Gad!"

XI

Primitive Rituals of the Wa-Chagga

It was some while before my strenuous efforts could calm the enraged Witherspoon. He was like a man possessed, his white hair flying madly about his head and his lips writhing in fury. But at last some measure of calm was restored in the close confines of our hut. Once he was a little cooled down, of course, Witherspoon saw that complaints and protests would avail us nothing. We must wait, as quietly and as patiently as possible, to see what the night's ceremony would bring. The poor distraught man struggled heroically to control his emotions and to limit himself to muttering and an occasional outraged "Harrumph!"

The waiting itself was torture, and we thought that no suffering the savages might impose upon us later, no matter how exquisite, could match this for its pain.

At one point late in the afternoon, Witherspoon growled an angry

"Harrumph." Of course he was right, a cup of tea would have been a blessing, but the savages, living in heathen darkness as they did, apparently lacked all forms of civility.

But finally we saw through the entrance of the hut that night had fallen, and I am certain that each of us wondered if he would live through this night to greet another day. I confess that I myself shuddered at an image that suddenly formed in my mind, that of my own name inscribed on the brass plaque in the foyer of the Adventurers Club. Was I never to see Pall Mall again? Was this where it would all end for Witherspoon and myself, and for the wronged Ngugi and his loyal brothers?

It was not long then before our captors entered the hut and ordered us out. We were herded together like cattle and driven through twisting ways between a dense scattering of huts until we emerged onto a vast open concourse at the center of a huge city—that is the only word for it—of similar dwellings.

What a spectacle greeted our eyes! I daresay that no civilized man, excepting Witherspoon and myself, has ever gazed upon the like.

Surrounding an enormous open space was what seemed the entire population of the wa-Chagga. Torches burned in a vast circle and illuminated the hideous scene as if with the very fires of Hell. On one side, to our right. the circle was composed of men, warriors all, in their full primitive regalia. decked out with the bones of wild beasts and with faces painted. Many, the older among them, seemed to be wearing about their necks the manes of lions. Each and every one carried a spear in his right hand and an animal-skin shield on his left forearm.

On the instant of our appearance within the circle, the men began beating their spears upon the shields and stamping their feet on the hard earth, setting up a cacophonous thunder.

The circle to our left was composed entirely of the wa-Chagga women. Although it pains me to do so, I must report, in the interests of this factual narrative, and for the insight the information may offer into the savage mind, that the women, every one of them, were shamelessly bare-breasted.

As if with one voice, Witherspoon and I both exclaimed, "By Jove!"

The far side of the circle fronted on a hut that was larger and grander in its details than any of the others, and it was toward this dwelling that our guards directed us.

"My father's house," Ngugi whispered to me as our little party crossed the open space. His voice revealed the seething anger his heart could barely contain.

We were brought to a halt facing the royal dwelling. Our guards indicated with grunts and gestures that we were to stand there and wait by ourselves, for they then retreated to join the ranks of men on our right.

The din of pounding feet and spears rose in volume to a fever pitch, and then the entire wa-Chagga tribe turned to its right and began a hopping little dance that slowly moved the entire population around the great circle until each person had returned whence he had started. This procedure took some minutes. The women, it seemed, threw themselves into this dance with a special passion. For the sake of thoroughness, it should be reported that the wa-Chagga women were surprisingly comely, and the swaying of their breasts produced in me a most unsettling sensation of distress.

Then the dance was at an end and the drumming of feet and spears suddenly stopped. It did not seem possible, but the silence that now enveloped us roared more loudly than had the primitive music.

"Make no move," Ngugi whispered beside me.

I discerned a movement in the doorway of the royal hut. A moment later we had our first view of the evil chieftain who was now about to proclaim himself a god. It had to be Kamala, for, even without Ngugi's choked exclamation, I knew it could be no other.

This giant savage embodied within his grotesque person the very darkest essence of Africa. I judged him to be near seven feet in height, a height that was crowned by an immense bald head out of which glared narrow yellowish eyes. His brown torso and huge bulging stomach were painted in white with stripes and circles. There was white on his face as well, and all round his mouth had been painted a gigantic double row of ferocious teeth.

He came slowly forward in the midst of his hushed population. He walked with a lumbering gait, his huge frame swaying from side to side with every step. Halfway between the royal hut and the spot where we stood, he came to a halt. Still swaying slowly from side to side, picking up each foot in turn and setting it down, he leaned forward as if the better to study us.

Ngugi, I was relieved to note, had taken up a position a little behind Witherspoon, so as to conceal his features from Kamala.

Then Kamala suddenly straightened to his full height and performed an action I have never otherwise seen enacted by a human being. He beat his great meaty hands upon his protruding stomach, which resounded like a drum, as if to say that he would devour all eight of us whenever the mood came upon him. His eyes and mouth had flown open as he did this, and I could not help but think that the mood would come upon him soon.

The time had come to act.

"Kamala!" I called out, and took a step in the direction of the giant.

At the sound of my voice, he stopped beating his hands upon his stomach, but I could see no change of expression on his face. What I did see was two normal-sized men—that is to say, merely six feet each in height—come forward and take up positions at either side of him.

"Kamala, hear me!" I called.

At that, the brute's eyes seemed to focus directly upon me. I prayed that my dialect would be clear enough for him to understand.

"My brothers and I come to you from a place far away. We come to you from the home of the gods, for word has reached us that you wish to proclaim yourself a god like us. Is this not so?"

The two henchmen held a hasty whispered conversation behind the brute's back, but Kamala himself warily grunted affirmatively in my direction.

"Well, then," I said loudly. "We come to bear you friendly greetings from all the gods, our brothers, but I must also tell you that we do not bear you good wishes on this occasion."

Kamala grunted again, angrily this time. A swipe of one of his huge paws behind his back instantly silenced the whispering of his lieutenants.

"That is right, Kamala," I called, emboldened by the effect my speech was having on him. "I hope that you can understand my words, Kamala, for we gods speak a higher form of language than that spoken by mere mortals like yourself. Listen closely, Kamala, let my words ring in your ears, and in the ears of all the wa-Chagga people."

I had them now, for a certainty, and thought I would solidify my position. Raising my right arm high to call for attention, I walked in a slow circle around our own little group, my gaze sweeping across the faces of every man and woman in the tribe. It had the right effect, for every single one of them took a step backward.

I returned to my position and faced Kamala once again.

"My words are these," I called out in my loudest tones. "Hear me, Kamala. The gods know that you mean to proclaim yourself a god this night. We have come from the place of gods to tell you that you shall not. The gods know that you mean to take a new wife this night, a wife whose skin is white like mine. We have come from the place of the gods to tell you that you shall not. The gods know that you rule the wa-Chagga people with a hand that is heavy and cruel and stained with blood. We have come from the place of the gods to tell you that you shall not."

I was silent then and left the brute to think things over for a minute. I felt Witherspoon's surreptitious touch on my back and heard his quiet "Harrumph." I appreciated that, for I was trembling with anxiety.

We waited to see how the giant would react. Ngugi whispered in my ear that the two henchmen were the same would-be politicians who had engineered his overthrow. Fury seethed in his voice.

"You!" Kamala called suddenly. "I have seen white faces before. You are no different from them, yet you say you are a god. And those others with you, their faces are brown like mine."

"Beware, Kamala, how you address the gods!" I called at once. "Impudence from a servant will not be tolerated. As for our colors, do you not know that a god may be any color he wishes? I wish, for the present, to be the color I am. My brothers wish to be the colors they are. I will not speak further on this question, for it is a foolish one."

Kamala, somewhat taken aback by my reply, now consulted at length with his lieutenants. They all displayed some consternation and uncertainty about how to proceed. Clearly, they had not often been visited by gods and lacked a protocol for the event.

"Kamala!" I called. "Cease your chattering and listen to me! My brothers and I have come from the place of the gods to perform a mission. We have come to gladden your heart with our presence only briefly, for our main task is to escort our sister back to her home among the gods. Bring her forth at once. The gods command this."

Kamala did not react as I had hoped. Instead, he took a swaying step forward and glowered at us, all the while beating his huge hands against his belly in a belligerent rhythm.

"You say you are gods," he muttered darkly. "Then you must prove it." Despite his scowling, I thought his challenge was lacking somewhat in conviction.

"The gods are not obliged to prove themselves," I answered him, "but I will do so this once because your mind is clouded by your own ambition. Prepare to be amazed!"

"And pray this works!" I whispered to my friends. "Ready?"

They formed a tight circle behind me, as we had planned, and Ngugi gave the signal.

I faced the giant savage once again.

"Kamala, hear this, for we will now give a sign that will prove our godliness to you."

Now I addressed the entire circle of the wa-Chagga people. "Let every man and every woman of twenty years or more come forward."

They hesitated for a moment but then, one by one, a few of the men stepped cautiously into the circle. Others followed at once.

"Hear me, people of the wa-Chagga!" I called. "The gods command you to search in your memory, search back to the time when Kamala became your king. Do not pretend that you do not remember, for the gods know that you do, and will be angry at the man or woman who tries to fool them. Search back now in your memory to that time. Remember the king who came before Kamala. Remember how you prospered under his leadership. Remember how he died of a sickness in his chest. Remember how that good and generous king had two sons."

The people were stirring uneasily now all round the great circle, and muttering darkly among themselves. A few, I noted, were even casting angry and suspicious looks in the direction of Kamala. If I could speak exactly the right words now, the tide would be turned. If I did not, our lives wouldn't be worth a brass farthing.

"Remember these things, O people of the wa-Chagga! Remember how evil men came to the boy Kamala in the night and plotted with him to make him king in place of the rightful heir. Remember how the other son, who should today be your king, was seized by those evil men and cast out from among the wa-Chagga to die in the heat of the jungle and the plain. Remember this boy's name. Remember Ngugi!"

They repeated the name, thousands of voices speaking it at once, and the chant rose into the night as if fired by the flickering flames of the torches. "Ngugi! Ngugi! Ngugi!"

"Hear me!" I called again, and the chant at once faded to a murmurous background.

"Your rightful king, Ngugi, was murdered by these evil men. Wait! Listen to me! He died a terrible death, too terrible for you to hear. But, seeing this, the gods came and gathered him to themselves and made him one of them as a sign of honor. Your rightful king, Ngugi, is a god! And, people of the wa-Chagga, he is come among you again!"

The murmuring swelled instantly to a roar.

"He is among you even at this moment. You will know his face. You will recognize his words. You will see that he is truly Ngugi, for he knows those things that only Ngugi could know. And when you see this marvel before you, your own king returned to your midst as a god, risen from the dead, you will bring down the false king and his evil followers and put Ngugi in his place and live in peace once again. Behold!"

I stepped aside quickly as Ngugi leaped forward.

Every wa-Chagga voice gasped.

"I am Ngugi, king of the wa-Chagga!" he began in a loud voice. Speaking rapidly, he told of his childhood, recalled famous lion hunts conducted by his father, reminded them of the habits of himself and his family, described features of the land thereabouts, all of this with great richness of oratory and a wealth of detail, his voice swelling with pride and confidence as he spoke.

The people were clearly amazed, for they recognized every word he spoke as the truth, verified by their own recollections.

"But I have yet another wonder to show you!" Ngugi cried. "For, behold, these are my half-brothers who were murdered with me. My three other half-brothers have remained in the place of the gods to see to my affairs there in my absence, but five of the eight are here with me now. Behold them, people of the wa-Chagga! Behold me, people of the wa-Chagga! Behold your rightful king, people of the wa-Chagga! In the name of all the gods, I command you to bring down the wicked mortal who has wrongfully taken my place!"

Barely had he finished this powerful speech when his five half-brothers each slipped a hand into his loincloth and brought forth the gleaming blade of a knife. This part of our plan had not been discussed beforehand, for we had thought to act in accord with the circumstances, and I myself was as surprised as the giant Kamala, who reeled backward several steps in fright. He immediately came up against his two lieutenants, who fell over, and the three went down in a tangled heap.

Nearly in the same instant, Ngugi and his half-brothers fell upon them with their knives, and the bloody deed was completed in a matter of seconds.

Ngugi rose and turned to face his people, his eyes bright with triumph. His half-brothers ranged themselves alongside. Speaking as if with one voice, the half-brothers raised their bloody knives in victory and cried out, "People of the wa-Chagga! Behold your rightful king! Behold Ngugi!"

And the people, their dusky features illuminated by the flickering torchlight, answered in return, the chant rising like a wave of sound around us.

"Ngugi! Ngugi! Ngugi!"

XII
A Captive Released

Savagery and bloodletting are ever terrible sights to behold, and although I have witnessed—as had Witherspoon and every other member of the Adventurers Club—acts of savagery in every corner of the globe, I think I have never seen worse than our eyes were witness to that night.

And yet, there was a kind of primitive justice in it. These may perhaps strike the reader as shocking words, but I write them only after a full measure of careful consideration. No Englishman could condone such actions, of course, but we are blessed with the gift of Christianity, with the model of a loving monarch, and with a benign system of government. Such savagery is alien to us.

The African, on the other hand, even when he gives outward evidence of civilization, is yet a creature of the bush. The refining influence of English society and customs has penetrated the surface of

Africa, it is true, but has yet to penetrate to the heart of the African. We can but pray that efforts will continue and even increase to bring the light of civilization into this darkest of continents.

In the case of Ngugi, he acted in accordance with his best powers of intelligence and his finest sense of justice. Translated into simpler terms, I mean that the fellow did the best he could. A savage himself, he killed his savage foe. It is nothing more than a beast of the jungle would do in like circumstances, and we would attach no blame to its action. Let the reader search his conscience, and let the matter rest there.

So it was that Ngugi triumphed and was hailed by his people as king of the wa-Chagga.

But another, equally pressing, matter was yet to be resolved.

"Ngugi," I said to him quietly when I could squeeze in among the warriors, former playmates and old friends all, who were happily congratulating him on his becoming both a god and a king. "Ngugi, you pledged us your aid in another matter."

At once he stepped aside from the warriors and looked chagrined. "Forgive me, Waterstone-Foyle," he said, "and you, Witherspoon. It is childish of me to celebrate my own victory and meanwhile forget a pledge to the very friends who helped me win it."

He turned to the painted warriors who surrounded us.

"Here, some of you," he cried, "run and fetch the woman with the white face who was to wed my brother this night. Bring her to me here."

At once, several fierce-looking bucks took to their heels and dashed away across the open space at the center of the village.

I took the opportunity, while we were waiting, to confer with Witherspoon.

"Harrumph," he said.

"Yes," I said, "I thought the same myself. Well, it is agreed, then. Assuming the poor little waif is in good health, we must tell Ngugi that we wish to leave at first light in the morning. Best to get away at once, I think."

"Harrumph," Witherspoon agreed.

"Well, that's settled, then. We shall request an escort of wa-Chagga warriors and a supply of stores to ease our way, that is all." I consulted my pocket notebook. "Yes," I said, "I thought so. If my calendar is correct, a ship sails for England in twelve days' time from Mombasa. We shall just have time to be on it."

"By Jove!" Witherspoon said with obvious pleasure. No degree of savage hospitality, after all, could match the warm and satisfying embrace of England.

But then we were distracted even from these pleasurable anticipations by a sight we had long been yearning to see.

A gang of warriors was walking toward us across the broad expanse of open ground. They were tall, each at least six feet in height, and painted about the face and body in the strange cabalistic way of the wa-Chagga. They were grinning, but they looked none the less fierce for that.

And walking in their midst was a little white slip of a thing. She was lovely and had somehow, through a captivity that must have seemed both endless and hopeless, managed to keep up her spirits. She walked with her head held proudly upright and her back straight, and the light of intelligence flashed brightly from her eyes. She made me proud to be an Englishman. Her features were finely molded and I thought her easily the handsomest young woman I had ever seen. She had contrived in some fashion to keep her clothing neat and clean, and she was wearing a very simple dress that looked most becoming on her, even in this primitive setting. But it was her eyes that held one's attention. They were large, and dark, and appeared to contain the very depths of the sea itself. She wore no decoration otherwise, but she needed none. She had those eyes.

She advanced confidently across the open ground and at last stood before us.

"Mr. Waterstone-Foyle?" she said. What a pleasure it was to hear English spoken by a lady.

"At your service," I said, and offered a proper bow.

"My guardian," she explained with a sad little smile, "spoke of you often and described you exactly. And you will be Colonel Witherspoon."

"Gad!" said Witherspoon.

"Thank you so much for rescuing me. My name is Mary Cantrell."

"Gad!" said Witherspoon again.

And that was that.

The wa-Chagga had already been prepared for a celebration and it was duly held throughout most of that night, albeit with its nature somewhat revised. Ngugi was as good as his word and we set out with a large escort first thing in the morning, negotiated mountain, jungle, desert, plain, and seacoast, met the ship we intended, which set sail on schedule, had a pleasant voyage, and were back in London within a fortnight, mission accomplished.

XIII
The Adventurers Club Once Again, and Some Final Thoughts

No joy on earth, I think, not even the joy of adventure, can match the pleasure of returning after a protracted absence to the hallowed precincts of one's club. At least, so it was for me upon my return to Pall Mall.

I set myself immediately to the task—not arduous, to be sure, but lengthy—of setting the experience down for the record. This is the account that I now set before the reader. It contains everything of essence about the expedition, with the exception of a few further comments I yet wish to make.

My only disappointments, apart from the sad loss of Carstairs and Reville, of course, were, first, that we had no time to collect botanical specimens, for in Africa one may catalogue new species simply for the trouble of bending over, and, second, that we had no opportunity to do any real shooting, other than for our meat.

Mary Cantrell spent only one night in London and set forth the next day for Ireland, where, she said, she had a number of distant relatives who would take her in. Witherspoon and I were sorry, naturally, to see her go off so soon, but we had the pleasure nevertheless of seeing her a free woman in England.

On our voyage through the Indian Ocean, the Red Sea, the Mediterranean, and the Atlantic, Witherspoon and I had ample opportunity to put questions to Mary Cantrell about her captivity. Through her, we learned a great deal about the ways of the wa-Chagga, information which will shortly be made available to scholars who make a study of such things. In the process of our questioning, aided by Mary Cantrell's straightforward replies, we were also able to learn a number of things that interested us more directly.

How had she managed to survive, for example?

Mary Cantrell's response to this was shy and a little self-deprecating, but it was quite clear to us, her attentive audience. The fact is that she had immediately won over the hearts of her guards, who did not share in the dark designs of Kamala and his henchmen. Those who were set to guard her treated her with every mark of respect and courtesy, and were even at some pains to bring her the choicest morsels of food from their own huts. Such was the influence this remarkable young Englishwoman had upon the natives.

Had she tried to escape before our arrival?

No. She had trusted in her guardian, poor Berresford, to reach civilization and get a message to us at the Adventurers Club. The certainty that we would come, she said simply, had been enough to sustain her.

And what, we asked of her, was the fabled treasure of Kilimanjaro, which men would guard with their lives?

Her answer to this was a little circumspect, for which we soon discerned the reason.

The treasure, it seemed, was twofold, part of it ancient, part of it only recently acquired. The first part of the treasure was Kilimanjaro itself, the majestic mountain whose head was hidden in the clouds, and which fed and nursed the wa-Chagga through all their lives. We had gathered some sense of this ourselves from the speech of Ngugi.

The other, more recent, part of the treasure of Kilimanjaro and of the wa-Chagga was, once we recognized it, easily explained. That part of the "legend," as it had come to our ears, was of very recent origin, a matter of months, in fact, or less. The wa-Chagga, even led as they were by the evil giant Kamala, had recognized a pearl, as it were, when they found one suddenly in their midst. And that pearl had been Mary Cantrell herself.

And now, upon reaching the conclusion of this narrative of adventure, I would ask the reader to contemplate this. It is my contention —and I know it to be the feeling of all members in good standing of the Adventurers Club—that despite the darkness that lingers still in their hearts, the wa-Chagga, and indeed all the native peoples of Africa, have it in them to attain, one day, the attributes of civilization. And I offer as evidence the fact that, upon coming into contact with one Mary Cantrell, they recognized the worth of her, for in the time she lived among them, the decent folk of the wa-Chagga had secretly hailed her as "the Queen of Kilimanjaro." It is the highest tribute I can pay these simple folk to say that, given the identical circumstances, an Englishman could not have expressed a finer or truer sentiment.